FATE'S INTERVENTION

A Mystery Novel

Ronald Lamont

KITSAP
PUBLISHING

KITSAP PUBLISHING

FATE'S INTERVENTION
First edition, published 2018

By Ronald Lamont

Copyright © 2018, Ronald Lamont

Cover photo by ThroughTheView via iStock
Author photo by Tara Templeton

Paperback ISBN-13: 978-1-942661-91-7

Published by Kitsap Publishing
P.O. Box 572
Poulsbo, WA 98370
www.KitsapPublishing.com

Printed in the United States of America

50-10 9 8 7 6 5 4 3 2 1

Acknowledgments

To my friends and family for their overwhelming support throughout this journey. To Amber Gravett whose invaluable feedback helps me remain within the narrative of the characters I am attempting to portray. To Kitsap Publishing for making it all possible. And to the communities of Gig Harbor, Fox Island, and Kitsap County, Washington for inspiring the locations herein.

"There is no greater sorrow than to recall happiness in times of misery."

- Dante Alighieri

Other Mystery Novels by Ronald Lamont

(excerpts enclosed)

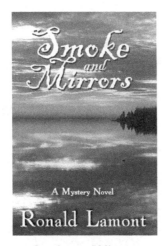

Smoke and Mirrors

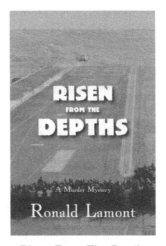

Risen From The Depths

Gig Harbor Register – July 28th

FOX ISLAND – The Chapel on Echo Bay was the scene of an apparent murder-suicide last night while celebrants were gathering for the Rehearsal Dinner of Miranda Davis and Colby Knudsen. The prospective bride and groom were unharmed; however, the victim was reported to be a member of the wedding party. It is unclear if the alleged perpetrator was also a member of the wedding party. Attendees at the event were inconsolable, with one person referring to it as "a tragedy of epic proportions". The names of the victim and alleged perpetrator have not been released pending notification of next of kin. Details concerning the manner of deaths are also not being released at this time.

1

July 17th – Gig Harbor Police Station

Officer Tyler McCord pulled the handset of his desk phone away from his ear. Still within his grasp he stared at the device as if a voice was going to continue to emanate, but the only sound reverberating from the speaker was a dial tone.

"Uh… that was weird," McCord commented with a scrunched-up face while continuing to hold the handset aloft.

Officer Nathan Buchanan, observing McCord's curious actions from a nearby desk, replied, "What's that?"

McCord placed the handset in its cradle. He turned toward Buchanan, "That was the manager of the Bridgeview Apartments."

"Reporting a break-in? Vandalism?" Buchanan queried.

"A strange smell… apparently coming from one of the units," McCord responded. "He tried the doorbell, knocking, even called the tenant's cell phone; but no response."

"Okay, I'm confused," stated Buchanan, "The guy is the *apartment manager*, correct?"

"Yeah."

"Then he obviously has access to the apartment; so why is he calling us before he goes in and checks things out for himself?"

"Two reasons," McCord explained… "The nature of the smell; and I told him not to."

"The nature of the smell?" replied Buchanan; "A gas leak? Meth lab?"

"Death."

Buchanan's eyes grew wide, "Death?"

3

"Well, his exact words were, *'the putrid stench of decay'*."

Buchanan's demeanor transitioned from shock to skepticism, "How would he know the smell of death?"

"That was my thought as well; and when asked he said having grown up on a farm near Silverdale he was familiar with the smell," McCord replied, "but it was the apartment number that prompted my directive."

Buchanan looked confused; McCord filled-in the blanks, "The Missing Person's Report we are waiting-out... you know, the forty-eight-hour requirement..."

"The *Eric* someone-or-other?"

"Yeah," McCord responded; "Eric Swenson." He grabbed his memo pad, "Number B-306... Bridgeview Apartments."

"The same unit the manager called about?"

"Yep."

"Son of a..." Buchanan started, "I guess that means we can *shit can* the forty-eight-hour criteria."

"You got that right."

2

A slim, mid-forties man, long straight hair pulled back into a ponytail, clad in beige cargo pants and a denim shirt, approached Officers McCord and Buchanan outside of Unit B-306, Bridgeview Apartments. "Officers," he said, extending his hand; "Tanner Hughes, the apartment manager... thanks for coming."

"Officers McCord and Buchanan," responded McCord as both of the Officers sequentially shook hands with Tanner.

"His girlfriend or fiancé or whatever called after he failed to show up for work... said he had been despondent and was concerned about him," Tanner commented as he inserted his master key into the deadbolt slot for Unit B-306.

"Any idea why she called *you?*" remarked McCord.

"She said you guys... the cops... couldn't look into it until he was missing for forty-eight hours," replied Tanner as he turned the key, "And she didn't want to wait."

Tanner turned the doorknob and cracked open the door – still nestled within the confines of the jamb. "I told her I couldn't go in without the tenant's permission unless there was something suspicious, but that I'd check to see if he was home... you know, maybe he was sick or something." Tanner turned to face the Officers, "But when I got a whiff of whatever's decomposing in there I figured I oughta call you guys."

A wisp of stench swept over McCord. "I can smell it now," he inhaled; then added with a look of suspicion directed toward Tanner... "But not when the door was shut."

"Ummm..." Tanner stammered, "Before I called you folks I unlocked the door; opened it just enough to stick my head in, and gave a yell; but

I didn't go inside... I swear."

"Wait here if you would, Sir," McCord directed to Tanner.

McCord and Buchanan stepped across the threshold. "Mister Swenson?" McCord voiced as he entered, "Gig Harbor Police Officers checking to see if everything is alright."

There was no response.

The Officers were now standing in a hallway – a coat closet to the immediate left, the hallway's path to the living spaces to the right.

Buchanan, standing near the coat closet, slid the bi-fold door of the closet open. A quick scan yielded a raincoat, a heavy winter jacket, and a long-handled umbrella. "Nada," Buchanan noted and turned away, leaving the closet door open.

"Mister Swenson?" McCord repeated as he ventured down the hall; Buchanan right on his heels. He stopped at the first doorway – a bedroom. He stuck his head in and looked around – nothing noteworthy within his line of sight. A simple sniff confirmed that it was not the source of the stench.

Dead ahead was a second doorway; this one opened up to the bathroom. Buchanan sidled past McCord to take a peek. He surveyed the space and then pulled back the shower curtain. He seemed perplexed. He glanced at the toilet and then back at the tub & shower.

"Anything in there?" McCord directed to Buchanan.

"Nothing more than a contradiction," Buchanan replied.

"A contradiction?" McCord queried as he approached.

"Toilet seat is down; but the tub is typical 'bachelor pad'."

"Hmm... so the girlfriend visits," McCord surmised, "but doesn't spend the night?"

"That's my take," said Buchanan, "Or she leaves early in the morning and showers at home."

"That wouldn't make sense on a weekend, though."

"Maybe he goes to her place on the weekends?" said Buchanan as he opened the cabinet beneath the sink. "Or not," he added as he pulled out a trash can and held it in front of McCord, "It's chock full of her stuff." He thought for a moment, "At least I assume it's hers."

"What's the inventory?" said McCord.

Buchanan rummaged through the contents… "Eye liner, moisturizing cream, lip gloss, a package of Mydol, a woman's razor, a toothbrush…"

"Now that I think about it," noted McCord, "the report did mention that his fiancé had broken off the engagement – said he took it pretty hard."

Buchanan opened the medicine cabinet, "None of her stuff in here."

McCord thought for a moment and then scurried off to the bedroom. "Nothing of hers in here, either," he said. He slid the closet door open; "That's interesting," he mused.

"What's that?" Buchanan loudly replied from the bathroom.

"All men's clothing here in the closet, but there's a row of empty hangers on one end."

"As if she took all of *her* clothes and either she, or he, tossed her other stuff… her toiletry items?"

"That's how it looks," McCord replied as he approached. He gave a head nod toward the hallway, "Let's get back at it."

The hallway had stopped at the bathroom and essentially made a left turn… a right turn for McCord and Buchanan exiting the bathroom. They continued their search in the new direction.

The intensity of the stench grew, and McCord noticed a doorway to his immediate left. He peered inside to discover the laundry room.

"Well, there's our source," McCord stated as Buchanan approached. "Have the manager come in, would you?" he added.

Buchanan went back down the hallway and motioned to Tanner. "We believe we've discovered the source of your concern," he uttered.

Tanner walked nervously toward the laundry room. He stuck his head through the doorway and exhaled. "Crap… that's Mister Brewster," he commented.

McCord wasn't sure if he heard Tanner correctly. "Mister Brewster?"

he asked.

"Yes."

"His dog is named Mister Brewster?" McCord sought clarification.

"He's a pug, actually," Tanner responded.

"Yeah, I can see that," said McCord, "Is there anything else you can tell us?"

"I heard that the poor little guy had been sick, but that's all I know."

Buchanan donned latex gloves and went in for a closer look. He scanned the dog over and stated, "I'm no expert, but I'm guessing he either died of old age or from whatever sickness he was suffering from."

"What makes you think that?" replied Tanner.

"He appears to be an older dog, and he looks undernourished," he paused and then pointed, "but there's plenty of food and water in his bowls."

"I see what you mean," Tanner nodded.

"Who leaves a dog all alone for an extended period of time; especially one who is old or sick?" commented McCord. "The whole *man's best friend* is supposed to work both ways," he shook his head in disgust.

"A shame," Buchanan noted.

"Well, he's evidence until we find out what's up with Swenson," added McCord. "Mister Hughes," he directed to Tanner, "You can either wait here or back at the entryway while we proceed."

"Understood," Tanner replied.

McCord and Buchanan moved on to the remainder of the apartment… the living room, kitchen, and dining area.

The hallway opened up to a living room on the left. It consisted of a sofa, coffee table, end table, reclining chair; and a flat-screen TV resting atop a small cabinet.

The kitchen was on the right side of the apartment. It was long and narrow. One wall contained the refrigerator, cabinets, sink, and dishwasher; the far end featured the stove. To the left was a long counter that separated the kitchen from the dining area. A number of stools on the dining area side graced the counter. One end of the counter looked to be a work station… pens, pencils, notepads, and the plug-in to a laptop.

The dining area consisted solely of a small table with four chairs; along with the stools that were tucked under the countertop.

From the vantage point of the Officers, they were finding nothing of note within the spaces that might provide any clues as to the whereabouts of Eric Swenson.

As they were about to wrap things up McCord noticed a small wastebasket near the workstation. Nestled within the basket were crumpled-up scraps of paper. McCord extracted the scraps from the basket and un-crumpled one of them. It read…

"I look into your eyes
Is it you or a disguise?
Do you ask the same of me?
Do we share the mystery?"

"What is it?" Buchanan relayed to McCord.

"Some kind of poem, I guess," McCord responded. He handed the scrap to Buchanan and then un-crumpled a second one. It was smaller than the first, but seemed to relate; it read…

"Do I share all that I feel?
Of my heart do I reveal?"

McCord handed the second scrap to Buchanan; who returned the first one to McCord.

"These aren't bad," Buchanan said after reading the second scrap. He looked directly over to McCord, "Why would he crumple them up and toss them in the trash?"

"Maybe they were written for his fiancé and when she broke off the engagement his hurt, frustration, or anger took over?" replied McCord as he mimicked the act of angrily crumpling up the paper and throwing it in the trash can.

"Makes sense," said Buchanan as he returned the second scrap to McCord.

"Mister Hughes," voiced McCord.

"Yes, Sir?" responded Tanner as he approached.

"Since you seem to know a lot about Mister Swenson's dog, and are familiar with his fiancé, does that mean you know Mister Swenson himself fairly well?"

"Not really," Tanner shrugged.

"So... nothing about any writings or poems or such?"

"Mmm... nope," Tanner shook his head.

"Understood," McCord replied. He took another look at the scraps, paused in thought, and once again eyeballed the scraps.

"Something on your mind?" Buchanan directed to McCord.

"I'm wondering if maybe there's something to this second piece," McCord held up the scrap.

"How do you mean?" asked Buchanan.

"Why is it ripped so that it is separated from the other one?" He placed the two scraps together – the ripped edges matched up perfectly. "It's as if he painstakingly tore it away from the first part of the poem."

"Good point," remarked Buchanan, "You'd think he'd just crumple-up the whole thing and toss it."

McCord stared at the two scraps; contemplating possibilities.

Buchanan gave McCord a moment, and then broke the silence... "So, what do you think, Mister Wizard?"

"Mister Wizard?" Tanner curiously chimed in.

Buchanan turned to Tanner and thumb-pointed toward McCord, "Officer McCord here has a knack for getting a feeling about a case," he explained. "If I could get him to give me some lottery numbers, or the ponies running this weekend out at Emerald Downs, I'd be looking at early retirement."

McCord looked toward Tanner. "Obviously he's exaggerating," he said with a head-nod Buchanan's way.

McCord refocused on the notes. "Maybe he felt betrayed," he continued… "The words, *'Do I share all that I feel… of my heart do I reveal'*… maybe he felt he had revealed something from the heart and instead of his feelings being reciprocated, what he got was a knife jammed right through it?"

"You sound like you're speaking from experience there," replied Buchanan.

McCord gave a quick glance toward Buchanan but remained silent. When his gaze returned to the scraps something caught his eye. He moved the scraps slightly to catch them in a different light. "It looks like there are dried droplets on here," he said as he positioned the scraps at a certain angle.

Buchanan leaned in to take a look. "Tears?" he said as he glanced back at McCord.

"Probably," replied McCord, "Let's bag it for the lab."

"I'm thinking we should also ask the ex-fiancé about it," said Buchanan, "Maybe she can shed some light?"

"Mister Hughes," McCord directed to Tanner.

"Sir?" Tanner replied.

"Someone from our Forensic Team will be stopping by to pick up the dog and, I imagine, his dog dishes… possibly more," said McCord, "Please steer clear of the apartment, and do not disturb anything, until they arrive."

"Understood."

"And if Mister Swenson shows up; have him, or yourself, contact us immediately."

"Will do."

3

Officers McCord and Buchanan trudged up the steps of a small bungalow in the 'Old town' section of Gig Harbor, just a stone's throw from the harbor itself. McCord rapped on the door.

A mid-twenties woman, professionally attired, auburn hair, opened the door. A look of dread appeared upon her face at the sight of the Officers.

"Heather Kincaid?" asked McCord as he and Buchanan held up their credentials.

"Yes," Heather replied.

"It's about Eric Swenson," said McCord.

Heather's knees began to buckle. She frantically barraged the Officers with questions… "Did something happen to him? I thought you couldn't look into his disappearance for forty-eight hours? Since it hasn't been forty-eight hours that means you found him and he's in the hospital or he's dead, right?! Oh my God!" she finished… burying her face in her hands.

"Whoa, whoa, whoa, ma'am," McCord held up his hand, "We are not here because we have bad news about Mister Swenson." He took a breath, "To be honest, we actually have NO news about him, except that he was not at his apartment."

Heather wiped her eyes, "But then why are you here?" she asked.

"Hopefully to get some answers," Buchanan chimed in.

Heather remained silent, but her demeanor spoke the language of confusion and bewilderment. She glanced back and forth between the Officers.

"Tanner Hughes, the manager of Mister Swenson's apartment

building, called *us* after you called *him*," McCord clarified. "He had checked out Mister Swenson's apartment per your request and was concerned after he noticed a strange smell."

"A strange smell?" asked Heather.

"It turned out to be Mister Swenson's dog," said Buchanan, "He was dead in his doggie bed in the laundry room."

"Mister Brewster is still there in the apartment?" replied Heather.

"I'm afraid so," said Buchanan.

"Eric said he was going to bury him out in the woods near a trail where they used to run."

"Well, for some reason that didn't happen."

"Poor little guy," said Heather, "I feel awful."

"Why is that?" McCord probed.

"The timing of it all was just..." she fought for the words, "Ugh."

"How do you mean?"

"Mister Brewster had had health issues for some time, but Eric didn't..." she struggled, "I guess he wanted to tell me, but we were in the middle of the talk I told him we needed to have... you know, where I said that I wasn't ready... right now... to get married."

"I think I get the picture," remarked McCord.

"After the shock of my calling things off, the first thing he said was, *"Mister Brewster just died and now you're canceling our wedding?"* And then his lip started to quiver and his eyes got all glassy." She took a deep breath and added, "I... I didn't know what to say. And now I feel horrible."

"I understand."

"And then he said, *"I can't take this! Everything I've ever loved in my life is gone! My life is over!"* Then he turned and walked away," Heather explained. "I tried to say something, but I couldn't find the words. I just stood there... silent... as he got in his car and drove out of sight."

"No offense ma'am, but his statements don't sound all that ominous," commented Buchanan. "Not to the extent of calling in a Missing Person's report."

"That wasn't the reason," replied Heather, "It was the text I received this morning in response to one I had sent after he failed to show up for work."

Heather scrolled through her cell phone and then handed it to Buchanan. The text read…

No more work, no more play. The light once bright now fades to gray. And the Reaper's scythe – it points the way.

Pierced through the heart, I've lost my will. My loyal companion, once swift, lies still.

The only one who would not betray; I shall join him now, "To the abyss!" I say. No one cares anyway.

Goodbye. Forever

"Hmm…" Buchanan murmured, and then handed Heather's cell phone to McCord.

McCord read the text and then returned the phone to Heather. "Do you believe he would actually do himself harm?" he asked, "Or do you think his statement was merely intended to gain sympathy… to get you to reconsider the wedding?"

"He used to say that his life would mean nothing without me. I thought it was simply a sweet gesture… a way of professing his love. In fact, I always replied, "Me too" – like all young couples in love do." Heather took a breath, "But after I read his text it makes me wonder what he might actually do."

"Did you try calling him after you received it?"

"Yes, but he didn't pick up."

"Well, there was no suicide note anywhere within his apartment, so that's a good sign."

Heather cringed at the word *suicide*, even though it had been used in a positive context. In her eyes Eric's suicide note was staring at her through the screen of her cell phone.

"Ms. Kincaid?" said McCord as Heather appeared to be lost in thought.

"Uh... yes?" replied Heather as she returned from her momentary fog.

"Something of note that we *did* find were scraps of paper crumpled-up in a wastebasket," McCord continued as he held up two small evidence bags containing the scraps.

"Wow; that hurts," said Heather as she examined the scraps.

"How's that?"

"Hearing that they were crumpled-up and thrown in the trash," Heather explained. She turned to the Officers, "They're from a song he had written for me."

She paused in thought, glanced at the scraps, and then looked toward the front door. "But it's also weird," she added.

"It's weird?" asked McCord.

Heather turned and walked away. McCord and Buchanan looked at each other... they weren't sure what to make of Heather's sudden departure.

Buchanan peered inside in an attempt to see where Heather had gone, but it was to no avail... she had disappeared into the shadows. As they were about to call out for her they heard footsteps approaching. Heather returned with a piece of paper in hand. It was similar to the scraps the Officers had shown her, but this one was in pristine condition.

"This is from the same song," Heather said as she handed the paper to McCord, "It was taped to my door when I got home the other day."

"What day was that?" replied McCord as he scanned what was written on the scrap; it read...

"Is it chance or fate?

I'm not sure that I can tell,

It's so early after all.

Is it chance or fate?

I guess only time will tell.

Will you catch me if I fall?"

15

"The day he disappeared," Heather replied.

"You mean… *the day before yesterday?*" responded McCord.

"Well… yeah," said Heather.

McCord contemplated both the scrap and the timing of its placement on Heather's door. He handed the scrap to Buchanan.

"Interesting," Buchanan said as he read the lines and then returned it to Heather.

"What do you think it means?" McCord asked Heather.

"I wondered the same thing when I found it," Heather replied, "but I have no idea why he stuck it on my door."

"I'm thinking it's more about the words themselves than the location he placed them."

Heather glanced at the scrap. "I don't know," she said, "Maybe wondering whether his future will be determined merely by chance? Or will it be left up to fate?"

McCord held out his hand; Heather handed him the scrap.

"Could be…" McCord replied as he once again scanned the paper, "Or he wanted to make *you* wonder."

Heather stood and pondered the notion, but she had nothing left to say except to pose a question, "So, you're going to do something, right?" she asked.

"Well…" McCord started, "It's not that simple, ma'am."

"What do you mean?"

"He hasn't committed a crime; and he's an adult," explained McCord, "If he wants to just up and disappear that's his choice…"

"So what are you doing here then?" Heather interrupted, "Just going through the motions to give the appearance that you're doing your civic duty?"

"I apologize, ma'am; but I wasn't finished."

Heather abruptly went silent and crossed her arms… giving McCord an *'okay, explain yourself' shrug.*

"The aforementioned freedom to disappear if he so chooses

notwithstanding, I agree that his text does appear to show a reason for concern," McCord explained. "With that in mind, can you forward that to me?" He handed Heather his card, "Here's my cell phone number."

Heather glanced at the card. McCord added... "The case number is written on the back."

Heather turned the card around and then back to the front. She focused on McCord's number, scrolled through her cell, and forwarded the text.

McCord noted receipt of the text, and finished with, "Thank you very much for your time, ma'am."

Heather wanted to believe that the Officers were committed to finding Eric, but she was not yet convinced. She responded with merely a half-smile and a nod.

4

Back at the Police Station, McCord and Buchanan perused the items of interest regarding the apparent disappearance of Eric Swenson. The Officers made a point of using the words *apparent* and *alleged* in regard to this case; after all, as Officer McCord had relayed to Heather, if Swenson wanted vanish off the face of the earth he was legally free to do so. What had the Officers perplexed; however, was the nature of the few pieces of evidence in hand: Were they riddles to be solved in determination of Swenson's ultimate fate? Or were they simply a plea to Heather's heartstrings… to get her to reconsider their breakup?

"So we've got the scraps… poem… song… whatever you want to call them," commented McCord.

"And the semi-cryptic, potentially ominous, text," Buchanan finished. "Although it's interesting how it rhymed throughout its entirety except the very end," he pondered.

"To be honest, that aspect has me more concerned than the rhythmic portions," McCord responded.

"Why is that?"

"The rhymes seem to be more about making a poetic statement, but the end… *goodbye forever*… has a finality of purpose."

"Hmm… I hadn't thought of that," Buchanan grimaced.

"Another item of note…" McCord added, "Don't forget about his pooch… his alleged *one and only loyal companion* that he left to rot on the laundry room floor."

"Oh yeah," Buchanan concurred. "I'm not sure what to make of that." He pondered the possibilities… "Maybe some unplanned event occurred which kept him from coming back to bury the dog?"

"Like what… an accident?"

"Something like that."

"Well, hospitals and clinics know to contact us if he shows up," replied McCord, "As does the apartment manager and his former fiancé, so those avenues are covered."

"What about his family?"

"There's no one but his grandmother – who raised him. She's in an Assisted Living Facility in Northern California… hasn't heard from him."

"But she's going to call if he contacts her or shows up at her place, correct?"

"Yep."

Buchanan nodded. "By the way," he said, "it looks like you guessed right about the one scrap."

"How's that?"

"The knife… well, *scythe*… through the heart."

"I suppose," McCord replied – not putting a lot of stock in his previous conjecture, "but the verse he posted on his ex's door must have a greater meaning than those he trashed. After all, he made a *specific point* of making sure to place that portion where she'd see it."

"I agree, but she didn't seem to have any idea what that might be."

"That's because she's looking at it through a narrow lens… one based on the original intent of the song," said McCord, "We need to try to see it from his perspective… his current state of mind."

"Any ideas along those lines?"

McCord looked at the verse, paused in thought, and replied, "Not yet."

"Well I've got one," beamed Buchanan.

"Really?"

"Not about the scraps or the text, though."

"Let's hear it."

"His cell phone," Buchanan replied as he held up a phone.

"Uh… that's *your* cell phone."

"I know," replied Buchanan, "I was just using it as a prop."

"Let me guess," McCord responded, "The GPS function?"

"You got that right," Buchanan grinned.

"I thought his phone was turned off?"

"Apparently he just turned it back on." Buchanan pointed to the monitor, "I've got a location here on the screen."

"So where is our 'not so missing after all' Mister Swenson?" said McCord as he peered at the monitor.

"Lookout Point," replied Buchanan.

McCord grew wide-eyed, "Are you kidding me?!" he stated.

"No… What?"

"The note…" McCord hesitated, "…and the text."

Buchanan's face scrunched up, "What about 'em?"

"The note ended with 'Will you catch me if I fall?'" replied McCord, "and the text referred to 'the abyss'."

Buchanan noted the connection; and had a disconcerting thought, "You don't think he's looking to take a header off of the Narrows Bridge do you?"

"I'm not going to sit around here and wait to find out," replied McCord as he stood up and headed toward the door.

"Aren't bridge jumpers under the jurisdiction of the State Patrol?"

"He's at Lookout Point; not the bridge," McCord replied. "Are you coming or not?"

5

Officers McCord and Buchanan pulled into the parking area adjacent to Lookout Point, a scenic vista overlooking the Tacoma Narrows... a strait of the Puget Sound that separates the Kitsap Peninsula from the City of Tacoma. Above and beyond the strait looms the majestic Mount Rainier – fourteen-thousand feet of breathtaking, snowcapped, beauty. Unfortunately for the Officers as they scanned the scene, Eric Swenson was nowhere in sight.

"GPS?" McCord asked Buchanan.

Buchanan looked at the screen of the Cruiser's laptop. "Blank," he said... "He must have turned his phone off."

"Damn," replied McCord.

The Officers exited their vehicle and walked toward the vista area; several onlookers shifted their vantage point from the scenery to the Officers.

"Excuse us folks," said McCord as the Officers approached the onlookers and held up a photo of Swenson. "Have any of you seen this gentleman within the last ten... fifteen minutes?"

A nervous teenager, barely old enough to drive, holding hands with his timid girlfriend, glanced at the photo. "We just got here," he feigned ignorance. His girlfriend smiled concurrence with her boyfriend; her braces reflecting the late afternoon sunlight.

Two very fit, athletically-clad, thirty-something women stretching following their jog across the bridge, gestured a wave McCord and Buchanan's way. The Officers approached – McCord holding up the photo of Swenson.

The women studied the photo, looked at each other, and then back at McCord. "I think we just passed him on the bridge," stated one of them. "He was leaning against the rail, staring off into space; and then glanced our way as we passed," added the other.

The women looked back toward the bridge – the Officers followed their gesture.

"I think that's him right there," said one of the women as she pointed, "about a third of the way across the span – in the red shirt."

"Thank you very much," McCord replied as he nodded.

McCord trekked to an area of the vista point away from the public, while keeping an eye on the man in the red shirt; Buchanan right on McCord's heels.

"What's the plan?" Buchanan relayed to McCord.

"Well, he hasn't placed himself in jeopardy… in harm's way… as of yet," replied McCord, "So I'm thinking we just go have a talk with him… see what's on his mind."

McCord and Buchanan made their way to the head of the walkway that spans the bridge and began a casual trek toward the man in the red shirt – whom they were hoping was, in fact, Eric Swenson. Pedestrians on the walkway curiously eyed the Officers as they approached and subsequently passed them by. McCord and Buchanan provided the pedestrians with obligatory smiles and gestures while they maintained their focus on the man. Ideally, the person of note would remain oblivious to his surroundings… in a world of his own… fixated upon the scenic waters of the Puget Sound.

As the Officers approached they noticed the man look straight down toward the water for an extended period. The Officers slowed their advance. The man then buried his face in his hands. His action provided the Officers an opportunity to get within a couple of feet of the man unseen, but it also gave them a new cause for concern: The state of mind of the gentleman leaning against the rail.

"Eric Swenson?" McCord inquired of the gentleman.

The man quickly spun around in surprise. "Why do you ask?" he said as he wiped his eyes.

Getting an up-close look, the Officers were sure they had found their man. "Officers McCord and Buchanan," McCord replied while holding up his credentials, "There are some folks out there looking for you... concerned."

"Yeah... well, as you can see... I'm fine," Swenson replied. He returned his gaze out toward the water.

"We read the note you left on Heather's door," commented Buchanan.

"They were lyrics," replied Swenson; still looking straight ahead.

"We also read your text to her," said McCord, holding up his cell phone containing the text.

Swenson glanced over at McCord's phone and then back toward the water. "I guess that makes you two *top notch investigators*... good for you," he said – continuing to look away.

"Your words about the Grim Reaper, having lost your will to live, joining your loyal companion who passed away, diving into the abyss... they were all rather disconcerting."

Swenson turned and glared at McCord, "First of all, I didn't use the word *'Grim',*" he replied. "And I didn't say that I lost my will *'to live'*, nor did I say anything about *'diving'* into the abyss." He pointed at McCord's cell... "You've got the text right there; why are you putting words in my mouth?!"

"I apologize," McCord responded, "That's just how it came across to us."

Swenson didn't respond.

"So what did you mean about joining your loyal companion?" asked McCord.

"About taking him out in the woods and burying him," said Swenson. "A little memorial near a trail where we used to go to run... *'to run the stink off'* Heather used to say."

"But you left him back at your apartment," Buchanan interceded.

"And you know this... *how?*" Swenson turned to face Buchanan.

"Like we said," McCord interjected, "Some people were concerned."

"Yeah, well… I haven't gotten around to it yet," replied Swenson. He turned back to face the water, "I plan on taking him later today."

"About that plan…" said McCord, "I'm afraid you'll have to pick him up at the city's Forensic Lab."

"What the hell?!" Swenson spun around and responded.

"You were missing… the dog was dead on your laundry room floor… we had no idea if foul play was involved or not…" McCord explained. "So the guys at the lab picked him up about an hour ago."

"Dammit, what are you doing invading my privacy and snatching up my dog?! I haven't done anything wrong! Just leave me alone!"

"Our intent was only to help find a missing person and make sure they were okay."

"As you can see I am not *missing*; and I'm doing just fine. So go away already."

"A couple more questions and we'll be out of your hair."

Swenson remained silent.

"Your lyrics asked *'will you catch me if I fall?'*, and your text talked about *'the abyss'* and ended with *'Goodbye Forever'*," noted McCord, "And here you are at the Tacoma Narrows Bridge… you can see why we might be a bit concerned."

"You're getting all spun-up for nothing; I come here all the time… it's my Zen place."

"So all of those seemingly ominous words…?"

"They were intended to be poetic. I'm a songwriter… a lyricist… you're taking things literally."

"But you also told Heather that *'your life is over'*," commented McCord.

"I was referring to my life 'here'… this stupid town where people don't give a rat's ass how they treat you… where promises and commitments mean nothing."

Swenson returned his gaze out toward the horizon. McCord looked at Buchanan and motioned a head-nod. The Officers moved back several paces to assess and discuss the situation quietly; and, hopefully, give Swenson some breathing room... an opportunity to take pause and reflect... to reconsider any notions that might end in tragedy.

"What do you think?" Buchanan said to McCord while continuing to keep an eye on Swenson.

"Like he said," McCord replied with a nod toward Swenson, "He hasn't broken any laws," then added, "and he has a reasonable answer to all of our concerns... even if I'm not necessarily buying all of them."

"Yeah, that was my thought as well," Buchanan said. He nodded back toward Swenson, "But do we just walk away with him still leaning against the rail? Or do we try to get him to leave?"

"If we pressure him to leave, which we technically have no legal stand to do so," replied McCord, "who says he won't come right back once we depart the area?"

Buchanan provided something of an obligatory nod of concurrence with McCord's statement, but he wasn't exactly paying attention – he was fixated on what lie before him: He had noticed that Swenson kept looking down toward the water and taking a deep breath; he'd grip the rail tightly, and then momentarily relax. *Was he running various scenarios through his head... contemplating his next move? Was he trying to talk himself into an act of desperation... to summon the courage to take one final, drastic, step?* Buchanan wasn't sure what to make of Swenson's posture, but it was troubling.

Buchanan decided to make an unplanned and possibly miscalculated move. He began walking toward Swenson, "Just so you know..." he said to catch Swenson's attention, "although virtually every person who has jumped off the bridge here died almost instantly, there have been two people who survived." He paused momentarily to let that information sink in, and then added... "But surviving a fall from here... well... it's a potentially horrific outcome."

McCord was shocked at this move by Buchanan; he had a *What the hell are you doing?* look on his face.

"You break almost every bone in your body, your face is mangled, you end up a paraplegic or worse – a quadriplegic, you suffer severe head trauma – possibly brain damage... maybe even end up in a vegetative state..." Buchanan continued, "What kind of life is that?"

Swenson looked straight down at the water – he couldn't believe survival from this height would be possible... not from the perspective of his current vantage point. His mood transitioned from ambivalence, to concern. He took a deep breath. "Yeah, well..." he started as he pushed himself away from the railing, "you guys can stop trying to play *hero*. Like I said, I'm just here to relax and enjoy the view."

Swenson turned and commenced a casual stroll back toward the head of the bridge... toward Lookout Point. The Officers remained in place while keeping an eye on Swenson – a strategic move to appear non-threatening while analyzing the situation.

Once a reasonable buffer-zone had been established, McCord and Buchanan commenced walking back toward their cruiser while continuing to maintain a bead on Swenson.

"You took one hell of a risk telling him about prior jumpers," McCord pointedly commented to Buchanan, "That little stunt could have pushed him over the edge... literally."

"Hey, it worked, didn't it?" Buchanan replied.

"This time," McCord shook his head.

As the Officers arrived at the parking area Swenson climbed into his car and drove away... toward Gig Harbor.

"Do we follow him?" Buchanan asked.

"I think we've done all we can at this point," replied McCord as the Officers climbed in their cruiser – Buchanan behind the wheel, McCord riding shotgun... "But we'll run it by the Captain when we get back to the Station."

Buchanan placed the shift lever in DRIVE – merging onto Highway 16 heading northwest.

6

Heather's cell phone rang. Her stomach twisted into a knot and her heart fluttered as she gazed upon the Caller I.D. – it was Swenson.

"Eric… where are you?" she spoke into the phone, "I've been worried."

"You called the cops on me?" Swenson tersely replied.

"I was just afraid that…"

Click – the line went dead.

Heather frantically hit 'redial' – the phone rang, and rang, and rang… until it went to voicemail.

Heather tried again - same response.

Her lower lip began to quiver… a tear rolled down her cheek.

She dialed her phone once again.

Ring… ring… "Officer McCord," McCord said into the phone as he answered.

"This is Heather Kincaid," said Heather, "I just got a call from Eric."

"You just got a call from Eric?" McCord mimicked Heather's statement aloud as he turned toward Buchanan. When Buchanan glanced his way McCord silently mouthed, "Heather."

"He was upset at me for calling the cops; and when I tried to explain he hung up on me," Heather replied, "I tried calling him back, but he's not answering."

"We did talk to him, ma'am," replied McCord, "And although he wasn't overly pleased to have us track him down, he came across as being of calm and stable mind."

"You talked to him?"

"Yes."

"And he was okay?"

"He gave us no indication that he was intending to do himself harm," McCord explained.

"Alright then," Heather replied, "Thank you for taking my concerns seriously... and for finding him."

"You're welcome, ma'am."

McCord hung up his phone.

Getting a gist of the conversation, Buchanan made an observation, "You didn't tell her we found him on the bridge."

"Are you kidding? Remember how she almost completely lost her mind when we showed up at her door?"

"Good point," Buchanan noted. "Well I guess that's that, huh?"

"Maybe..." McCord replied. He began to manipulate the cruiser's laptop.

"What's up?" Buchanan said with a glance toward McCord while keeping an eye on the road.

"Seeing what our potential bridge jumper is up to," McCord replied while he typed and scrolled via the keyboard.

"Hopefully he's either heading home," said Buchanan, "Or swinging by the lab to pick up his dog."

"Dammit!" said McCord as he stared at the laptop... "He's back at the bridge!"

Buchanan did a quick check of his surroundings and engaged the cruiser's flashing lights. Up ahead was the exit from Highway 16 to Olympic Drive NW. Buchanan took the exit, turned left on Olympic Drive, crossed back over Highway 16, and took another left to the onramp – returning to the highway, heading southeast.

"You got a plan?" Buchanan inquired of McCord.

"Trying to keep him from doing something stupid," McCord replied. "How to do that?" he paused, "Not a clue."

"I'll keep my mouth shut this time," Buchanan lamented.

"That would be a good idea," McCord scowled.

Buchanan wheeled into the parking area near the head of the bridge.

He spied Swenson's car and made a beeline toward it while McCord surveyed the surroundings.

Swenson's vehicle appeared to be empty as Buchanan pulled up next to it. McCord was the first to jump out of the cruiser; he peered inside Swenson's car just to be sure – nothing.

Buchanan joined McCord as they scanned through the sea of onlookers at Lookout Point – no sign of Swenson. Their vantage point shifted to the bridge – no person off in the distance wearing a red shirt.

"Dammit!" said McCord, "Where the hell is he?"

Buchanan had a disconcerting thought, "You don't think he jumped, do you?"

McCord scanned the span of the bridge with binoculars. "Seems unlikely," he said, "There would be a crowd of people at the rail looking toward the water, pointing, and flagging us down."

"Holy shit!" Buchanan pointed toward the head of the bridge span, "It looks like someone's walking on the tubular catwalk portion of the bridge suspension!"

McCord shifted his line of sight via his binoculars. "Son of a bitch," he said, "It's Swenson; he threw on a sweatshirt."

"Purposely trying to keep us from spotting him in his red shirt?" responded Buchanan.

"Don't know and don't care at this point," replied McCord – still eyeing Swenson via his binoculars. "Aww shit!" he added, "He's starting to ascend the suspension; toward the tower."

The Officers ran to their cruiser, engaged the flashing lights and siren, and burned rubber as they raced to the bridge.

They pulled up next to the head of the suspension-portion of the bridge, blocking-off the far right lane, lights still flashing.

Prompted by the sound of the siren, Swenson momentarily ceased his ascent. He turned back to the sight of McCord jumping onto the catwalk, followed by Buchanan. He picked up his pace toward the tower, but with each step forward the steeper the angle of the catwalk grew – he was now fighting both gravity and the slickness of the steel-tubed catwalk. He looked back – McCord and Buchanan were gaining on him.

McCord was focused on the catwalk and his own forward momentum as he commenced his ascent, but Buchanan noticed Swenson eyeing the two Officers, "Mister Swenson… Stop!" Buchanan yelled.

McCord stopped and looked up toward Swenson.

Swenson looked right past McCord and directly at Buchanan, "Is this high enough for you now?!" he yelled.

Buchanan turned to McCord – his eyes spoke the language of regret. "Crap…" he exhaled, "We should probably call for a suicide negotiator, don't you think?"

"And the State Patrol," McCord replied.

Buchanan broke out his cell phone; McCord resumed his trek… as did Swenson.

The situation was becoming dire; courtesy of physics and the limitations of the human body. Keeping one's balance while walking along a steel tube with only the aid of a wire cable running parallel to, and a few feet above, the tube was difficult enough. But as the angle increased, the 'trek' was becoming more of a 'climb', and Swenson found himself grasping for the suspender cable bands that ran vertically down to the bridge deck every few feet along the 'catwalk' to hold himself in place. He looked back – McCord was closing the gap.

"Get back!" Swenson yelled, "Or I'll jump right now!"

McCord ceased his ascent. "Come back down and let's talk this out," he pleaded.

Swenson remained still. *Was he considering McCord's offer?* No such luck; he was merely resting. He had an endgame in mind, and he was going to make sure it would come to fruition… in one manner or another. He resumed his climb. McCord recommenced his pursuit.

The ascent was taking a physical toll on Swenson. It was like trying to make one's way up a slippery-slide, except that 'the slide' was a round tube, hundreds of feet long, with nothing to pull yourself along except thin coiled wires that were ripping your hands to shreds. His legs were growing weak, but that paled in comparison to his arms, which had gone beyond the point of fatigue and were approaching the point of failure. His grip was starting to fail as well; with the periodic suspender cable bands being his momentary savior as he approached the tower.

McCord was suffering similar stressors. His saving grace was his excellent physical fitness, and the gloves he was wearing that both aided his grip and kept his hands from being shredded by the wire cables.

Buchanan had returned to the bridge deck and was awaiting the arrival of the State Patrol, EMTs, and the suicide negotiator. As he looked up toward the tower with his binoculars he realized that there was likely nothing the negotiator could do; not unless he or she was going to be dropped off at the top of the tower by helicopter.

Buchanan continually followed McCord and Swenson's climb; periodically switching between an up-close view via binoculars, and the perspective provided by the naked eye in order to gauge their proximity to the tower. His stomach was in knots as he tracked the chase; fueled by the thought that he was likely responsible for this dire situation. His concerns were twofold: He had essentially goaded Swenson into taking this drastic action… inferring that a leap from the bridge deck would not be sufficient to achieve his goal of suicide; and he had subsequently put his partner's life in danger. It would be bad enough if Swenson took the ultimate leap; but if McCord took an unfortunate and deadly misstep, or worst-case-scenario Swenson decided to take McCord into the frigid waters of the Puget Sound with him, Buchanan wasn't sure how he could live with himself.

Swenson was nearing the point of exhaustion. At this point the only thing that was keeping him going was his resolve, and the fact that he was also nearing the top of the suspension cable… his ultimate goal of standing atop the tower. What he failed to realize; however, was that McCord had closed the gap such that he could almost reach out and grab him.

Swenson was struggling to drag himself onto the tower when he noticed McCord just below. He was so startled he almost lost his grip. "Geezus, you scared the hell out of me!" he gasped as he noticed McCord directly underneath him. "Go away!" he kicked.

McCord wanted to roll his eyes at the irony, "*Here he is tempting fate… apparently ready to throw himself off a bridge; yet he is frightened when he almost slips and falls after being spooked,*" he thought to himself. On the other hand, it told McCord that perhaps Swenson was not truly ready to embrace the prospect of certain death that awaits such a plunge from this height, but instead may be simply looking to make a statement… to garner sympathy… to get Heather to reconsider. Another notion popped into McCord's head: Swenson being startled at his near fall could have been nothing more than his natural instinct to catch himself from falling; and McCord knew all too well that a purposeful act trumps instinct. At this point McCord held out hope that Swenson's near-fall might have scared some sense into him.

Swenson crawled onto the top of the tower and flopped down on his stomach – he was exhausted. He wanted to rest, but he had Officer McCord to deal with, who was now pulling himself onto the tower as well.

"Stay away from me!" Swenson yelled… his voice starting to crack while he gasped for air. He began to bear crawl his way toward the opposite end of the tower.

"Take it easy," McCord replied, "I just want to talk."

Swenson spun around to a sitting position – his hands behind him, holding himself up – barely. "I dedicated my life to her! I made a promise!" he exclaimed. He started pushing himself backwards on his buttocks, "SHE made a promise!"

"Yeah, I get that," McCord replied, holding up his hands in a STOP gesture. "But didn't she say that she just wasn't ready NOW… which could mean there's still a future for you two?"

"I'm not an idiot! I saw the signs... I knew something was up!" Swenson glared.

McCord remained silent; figuring his best bet would be to allow Swenson to vent... to get it all out.

"Working late all the time... after-work meetings with her boss... so-called 'business trips' where I was never invited..." Swenson continued as he began to choke up.

"Some people have demanding jobs..." McCord started.

"What the hell do you know?!" Swenson cut him off... "Mister tall, dark, and handsome cop in his fancy uniform impressing all the ladies..."

"Hey, it may not seem like it," replied McCord "but I've been in your shoes."

"Don't give me that crap! I know how you guys work... feed the poor sap some line of bullshit in order to make some kind of connection... to get them to let their guard down."

"Look," McCord held out his hands, "I'm not a negotiator full of B.S. lines to throw at you; I'm just an everyday cop looking out for your best interests."

"Hah!" Swenson pointed at McCord, "There it is!"

McCord was confused, "Pardon?" he replied.

"Your well-trained and properly-chosen words," Swenson mocked while moving his head from side to side. "You can't even say bullshit... you have to be all prim and proper with quote-unquote B.S.," he gestured with air-quotes.

"Fine," McCord retorted, "I'm not full of bullshit lines."

"Wow, the spit-polished cop said a bad word," Swenson mocked. "And if you're truly looking out for my best interests then you'll get the hell out of here and leave me alone."

"You know I can't do that," McCord responded and crossed his arms... a stance that implied he wasn't going anywhere.

Swenson, still sitting on the surface of the tower, grabbed one of the wire cables with his left hand and stood up. He wobbled as he struggled to gain his footing – McCord made a quick jerking motion… ready to grab Swenson if he started to go over the side.

"Hold it right there," Swenson directed as he steadied himself.

McCord returned to a non-threatening stance.

"So, let's hear it," said Swenson.

"What's that?"

"Your so-called story," he explained; "Where you were in my shoes."

"Several years ago I met this gal," said McCord, "We hit it off immediately… similar interests, goals, and dreams for the future. She was smart, giving, affectionate… she pretty much spoiled me. And her wit, her sense of humor… we laughed our asses off."

Swenson's mood was transitioning from smartass to curiosity, "So… what happened?"

"She always spent the weekends at my place, so she had some clothes, makeup, perfume, and other things that she left there," McCord explained. "Then one Saturday after we got back from a picnic she said she wasn't going to stay that night because she was getting together with a girlfriend early the next morning. No big deal, right? Except that she packed up all her stuff… everything that she had always left at my place."

"You fucking liar!" Swenson screamed as he broke into tears, "Heather told you that story about us, you lying bastard!"

"Sir, I am telling you the absolute truth," McCord pleaded.

"That's bullshit; you're playing me just like she did!" Swenson retorted. "Making excuses… saying she's not ready… turning and walking away; all while adding to my misery by talking about the great times we *used to* have… *past* tense. She might as well have been delivering my eulogy," the tears streamed down his face.

"I'm sure that was not her intent."

"Dammit!" Swenson began bawling incessantly and put his head in his hands.

McCord saw an opening and jumped Swenson – tackling him to the deck of the tower.

"Get away from me!" Swenson shoved. But he didn't realize that he had backed up near the tower's edge and rolled right over the side. "Aaaahhh!" he yelled as he reached out to grab one of the wire cables encircling the tower. McCord immediately grasped Swenson's other arm.

"Hang on... I've got you," said McCord as he struggled to maintain his grip. He had an unfortunate realization: Both he and Swenson had physically exhausted themselves climbing the suspension cables to the tower. Would they have anything left?

"Just let me go!" Swenson sobbed as he let go of the cable wire – McCord's grip on his other arm being the only thing keeping him from a fall to his certain death; and that single thread was but mere moments away from unraveling.

McCord realized that he was going to need Swenson's help to save him; if Swenson made any effort to push himself away it would be impossible for McCord to overcome Swenson's weight and inertia.

"I swear that the story I told you is true; Heather didn't say anything about your breakup... not a word," McCord pleaded. "She told us she was worried about you; that she didn't want any harm to come to you."

"You're lying," Swenson mumbled.

McCord tried to think of something... anything that he could say to get Swenson to change his mind. And he had to think quickly – he could feel his grip beginning to fail. "She saved your note," he blurted out.

Swenson looked up, "My note?"

"Your song lyrics that you left on her door," McCord replied, "She held it close to her heart as she brought it out for us to see."

"She did?"

"Yes. Now come on; help me," McCord said as he started to pull on Swenson's arm.

Swenson reached back up with his free hand and grabbed the wire cable. He then tried pulling himself upward.

McCord began to pull Swenson toward him with all his might. "Aargh!" he yelled-out like an Olympic Weightlifter as he dragged Swenson up to armpit-level on the edge of the tower.

McCord took several deep breaths while he still had hold of Swenson's right arm. "Now I'm going to hold onto your right arm with my left hand, and I want you to quickly let go of the cable," he nodded toward Swenson's left hand, "and grab my right hand, and I'll pull you in."

Swenson released his left hand's grip from the wire and immediately grabbed McCord's awaiting hand. They both let out a yell as McCord dragged Swenson back onto the tower.

Now safely on the tower, the two of them fell limp – totally exhausted.

Something caught McCord's attention out of the corner of his eye – it was someone climbing onto the tower… he was wearing a rescue harness, with two more harnesses draped over his shoulders.

"Thank God!" McCord collapsed.

Dusk had swallowed the late afternoon sky. The silhouettes of what resembled a three-person chain-gang slowly made their way down the bridge's suspension cables. Officer McCord was in the lead, Eric Swenson next in line, with the Rescue Officer bringing up the rear. Clad in harnesses with dual straps and clasps... one clipped around the left cable wire, the other around the wire to the right... it was a slow, methodical, monotonous trek: Baby-step a few feet down the tube until the clasps were stopped by the vertical cable bands, unclip one clasp, reconnect it on the other side of the cable, unclip the opposite clasp, reconnect it on its associated cable, take a few more steps, and repeat the process through the entirety of the descent.

The trio was near the end of the descent before they realized what they were walking into – a bridge deck lit up like the Las Vegas Strip: Red, blue, orange, and white flashing lights from a multitude of emergency vehicles fighting each other for attention; spotlights from police cruisers illuminating the walkway; and the camera lights of a television news crew. The latter had McCord concerned; the thought of a distraught man whom had just escaped a brush with death, particularly one of his own doing, being bombarded and essentially interrogated by a news station looking for ratings, did not sit well. He realized he was being a bit cynical concerning the news crew's presence... just like him, they had a job to do; but his primary concern was the well-being of Eric Swenson.

McCord stopped in his tracks and turned around to face Swenson, but he hadn't considered that Swenson might be looking down to carefully track his footing as he negotiated the tubular path. Swenson was startled and stumbled as he literally ran into McCord; placing a death grip on the wire cables.

"Sorry," said McCord upon impact, "I should have warned you guys that I was stopping." The Rescue Officer gave McCord a nod; Swenson looked stunned as he got his first glimpse of the frenetic activity below.

"You okay?" McCord directed to Swenson.

"Uhh… I don't know," Swenson replied in a disheartened tone.

"We're not going to let you get caught up in all of that brouhaha," McCord nodded toward the sea of flashing lights. "Stick close to me and keep your head down."

When the trio got close to the end of the suspension Buchanan was on the bridge deck ready to help them down. "Hey Nate," McCord relayed to Buchanan, "Grab me a ball cap, would you?"

Buchanan disappeared to his cruiser and jogged back with a GHPD cap in hand. McCord knelt down as Buchanan reached up with the cap. McCord handed the cap to Swenson, who had been covering his face. "Pull this down low," McCord directed to Swenson as he handed him the cap. Swenson complied.

The news crew's camera lights were blinding as McCord stepped onto the bridge deck – Swenson hugging him like a passenger on the back of his Harley. McCord held up his hand to block the lights. Buchanan and two EMTs joined the trio to circle the wagons. The posse now surrounding Swenson, they walked him to the EMT van. McCord shut the doors and the EMTs drove away – getting Swenson to the hospital for a medical and mental evaluation. McCord faced the cameras and microphones.

"I'm here with Officer…" reporter Danielle Stevenson started as she placed the microphone in McCord's face.

McCord knew the drill, "Officer Tyler McCord; Gig Harbor Police Department," he replied.

"Officer McCord," Danielle said, "How does it feel to be a hero?"

McCord smiled, "I'm no hero; just trying to help a distraught young man who got himself into a precarious situation." He paused and then added, "Just doing my job."

❖ ❖ ❖

"My hubby the hero," McCord's wife Kayla playfully elbowed him while the two of them were sitting on the sofa watching McCord's interview on TV. "Oh, and Mister Humility, too," she poked him teasingly after his 'Just doing my job' statement.

McCord started to laugh as he attempted to block Kayla's pokes while simultaneously pointing at the screen, "Wait... there's more," he said.

❖ ❖ ❖

"Officer McCord," reporter Danielle spoke into her microphone, "How was it that you were in a position to rescue this distraught young man; did you just happen to be in the area and stumble onto the scene?"

"No ma'am," McCord replied, "The gentleman is a Gig Harbor resident and had been reported missing." He pointed toward Buchanan, "Officer Buchanan and I traced his movements to Lookout Point. In fact, it was Officer Buchanan who noticed the gentleman climbing onto the bridge suspension."

Danielle glanced at Buchanan and then back to McCord, "Then what happened?" she asked.

"He... the gentleman... started climbing the suspension cables, so I went up after him while Officer Buchanan contacted the State Patrol," McCord paused and clarified... "They have jurisdiction over the bridge itself and any potential jumpers."

"But you didn't wait for the State Patrol or a rescue team," Danielle probed.

"Officer Buchanan and I felt the situation was dire enough that action had to be taken immediately. I went up after the gentleman while Officer Buchanan coordinated with the State Patrol to get the bridge closed-off."

"What was the importance of closing-off the bridge?"

"The gentleman could have fallen at any point once he started climbing and, instead of heading toward the water he could've landed on the bridge deck, potentially injuring innocent pedestrians on the walkway, or drivers crossing the span."

"And you weren't concerned about your own personal safety?"

"To be honest, I didn't really think about it at the time."

"Somehow that doesn't surprise me," Danielle replied, "Thank you Officer."

"You're welcome," McCord responded.

The camera shifted back to Danielle, "And there you have it," she stated, "A potential tragedy averted thanks to the heroic efforts of two Officers from the Gig Harbor Police Department." She closed out her report with, "Danielle Stevenson – Channel Five News."

❖ ❖ ❖

The news program focused on the anchorman in the studio, "That was earlier this evening," the anchorman reported. "And we have an update to the story. The distraught young man has been tentatively identified as Eric Swenson, age twenty-five, a resident of Gig Harbor. He is being held overnight at Saint Anthony's Hospital for a mental and physical evaluation. We wish him well."

McCord sat on the sofa in disbelief, "You've got to be kidding me!" he roared at the television screen.

Kayla was both surprised and concerned at her husband's sudden mood change, "What is it?" she said.

McCord turned to Kayla while simultaneously flailing toward the television, "This kid was so close to the breaking-point that he was ready to throw himself off a bridge; the last thing he needs is all of the attention this is going to bring."

"Maybe all of the kind thoughts and well-wishes he's likely to receive will help in his recovery?"

"With social media these days? You know that for every dozen people providing words of support and encouragement there are always some jerks who will tease, taunt, and berate him."

"Yeah," Kayla sighed, "I hadn't thought of that."

"Let's just hope that the medical professionals, his family, or friends can provide some kind of support system... a safety net around the guy; otherwise, well... I don't even want to think about the potential consequences."

8

July 18th

"Hey Ty, did you happen to read the News Tribune this morning?" said Buchanan as McCord walked into the Police Station.

"Can't say that I have," McCord responded, "I'm guessing there's something in there about our little adventure yesterday?"

"You should read it, it's pretty good."

"I think I got enough from the news last night."

"There's speculation about an awards ceremony."

McCord shook his head, "You know I'm not into all that 'pomp and circumstance'."

"It makes for a nice photo-op."

"If I was looking for photo-ops I'd have chosen a different line of work."

Buchanan smiled, "Good point."

McCord reflected for a moment, "On the other hand… the positive press from the news media might have kept me from getting a reprimand."

"A reprimand?"

"Going after Swenson on the suspension cables without backup or safety gear."

"I see what you mean," Buchanan concurred.

"And speaking of Swenson… any update on him?"

"He was released from Saint Anthony's early this morning," Buchanan replied. "His first stop was the Lab to pick up *Puggy Brewster*," he added with a grin.

"Good one," replied McCord, "I can't believe I didn't come up with that nickname."

Buchanan's grin subsided. "Anyway," he started, "Not to get all weird, but you saved *both* our asses yesterday."

McCord looked confused, "What're you talking about?"

"Swenson's ass… along with mine."

"Yours?"

"I'm the one who goaded him into climbing the tower."

"You don't know that."

"Sure I do; he specifically looked right at me and said *is this high enough for you now?*"

"Perhaps; but on the flip-side, if he didn't decide to climb the tower then maybe he jumps from the bridge deck as soon we leave and now we're talking about a *floater* instead of a guy who's still walking upright?"

"Hmmm…" Buchanan conceded, "I guess I hadn't considered that possibility."

"Yeah, so quit beating yourself up."

Buchanan shrugged.

"So hey, that article in the Tribune," said McCord, "It didn't call out Swenson by name, did it?"

"Nope."

"Well, that's one saving grace; but probably moot thanks to the news stations."

"How's that?"

"The damn TV news guy last night 'tentatively'," McCord replied with air-quotes, "identified him."

"So much for keeping one's identity hidden when you're in a fragile state of mind."

"Exactly," McCord grimaced.

The sound of shoes shuffling along the carpet caught McCord's attention.

"Well, well, well... our local heroes," stated Police Captain Denise Prescott as she approached. "Working on your report, I assume?"

"Hey Cap," replied McCord.

"Yes, ma'am," Buchanan added.

"Just filling in the details around the initial debriefing we gave you last night," McCord relayed to the Captain.

"Make sure you leave no stone unturned," noted the Captain.

"Understood," replied McCord.

The familiar sound of a buzzer rang out; followed by an equally-familiar chime and *click*. An unexpected visitor entered the Station. The Officers stood up to greet her.

"Mayor Duvall," said Captain Prescott as she reached out to shake hands.

"Sorry to drop in without prior notice," stated the Mayor, "I just wanted to thank Officers McCord and Buchanan for their efforts yesterday."

"You're welcome to drop in any time, Madame Mayor," replied the Captain.

The Mayor pooh-pooh'd such a notion, "I appreciate the thought, but the last thing you folks need are politicians showing up on a routine basis." She extended her hand to the Officers. "You gentlemen showed us what the phrase to *serve and protect* truly means," she said as she shook hands with Buchanan and then McCord. "Words like those often get lost in campaign slogans."

McCord started to open his mouth, but the Mayor cut him off, "And don't say you were just doing your job," she winked, "Even if it's true."

McCord smiled, "Yes, ma'am... thank you."

"I saw you on the news descending the bridge tower," added the Mayor, "That would have scared the hell out of me; although not as much as climbing the suspension without a harness."

"Yeah, that probably wasn't the smartest move on my part," McCord replied as he glanced over toward Captain Prescott – the Captain giving him a look of concurrence with his assessment.

"Sometimes you've gotta do what you've gotta do," said the Mayor.

"Yes ma'am."

"There's been talk of an awards ceremony, but I'm getting the impression you'd prefer to avoid such a spectacle?"

"To be honest, ma'am," replied McCord as he nodded toward Buchanan, "Our thoughts are that such a public display might be difficult for Mister Swenson – the distraught gentleman who almost took the ultimate leap."

"And it wouldn't feel right for us to be involved in a ceremony without Mister Swenson," Buchanan added.

"Well, I can't argue with that," replied the Mayor. "I'm sure the Captain and I can come up with something appropriate," she nodded toward Captain Prescott.

"Yes, ma'am," the Captain replied.

"Thanks again," said the Mayor as she raised her hand and exited the building.

Captain Prescott looked toward McCord, "I guess that means you're off the hook... this time," she said.

"Are you talking about the awards ceremony?" McCord wondered, "Or my lack of safety gear when I went after Swenson?"

"Both," the Captain replied.

He stared at the backs of his hands – they were shaking almost uncontrollably. A gauze bandage wrap covered all but his thumb and fingers. He turned his hands over – palms up. Staring back at him were rust-colored stains where blood had seeped-through the gauze and dried. His hands were throbbing, but he was feeling no pain – the medics had made sure of that.

He dropped his hands to his sides and slowly looked up at the reflection in the mirror, "Geez, you look like shit," he said aloud. Red, glassy, puffy eyes; streaks of dried tears lined his cheeks; matted hair like a mangy mutt. "No wonder she walked away, you pathetic loser," the man in the mirror replied.

He turned and began a zombie-like shuffle out of the bathroom and toward the bedroom. "Dead man walking," he said as he trod.

He flopped down on the bed face-first…

10

"I thought cops only got stuck with desk duty after they were involved in a *shooting?*" Officer Buchanan complained to Officer McCord.

"What are you, a rookie?" McCord responded, "You know we always have to fill out a report after *any* major event."

"Yeah, I know, but I hate this part of the job," Buchanan sighed. "If I wanted to be a desk jockey for a living I'd have studied to be an accountant."

"Says the guy who can't even fill out a 1040EZ on his own," McCord shook his head.

"Oh, we've got a comedian in the house."

McCord showed off his pearly-whites.

"Okay, I'll get back to the subject at hand," said Buchanan.

McCord nodded.

"So, here's something interesting," said Buchanan.

"About the report?" McCord queried.

"Not exactly," replied Buchanan, "But potentially related."

"Let's hear it."

"I read an article online about 'Despair Deaths'," Buchanan said with air-quotes.

"Despair deaths?"

"Deaths due to drugs, alcohol, and suicide."

"Hmm... I've never heard that term before."

"I hadn't either," replied Buchanan, "but apparently that triad is killing more Americans than ever before."

"A sad state of affairs," McCord lamented.

"True; but at least we made a difference in this one instance."

"Yeah," McCord concurred, "Like the Captain says, any day that a life is saved is a good day."

"The article went on to say that there's evidence of a relationship between them... that you can't just look at suicide and not consider drugs and alcohol as part of the equation," Buchanan continued. "The thought being that some of those at risk might not be medicating *physical* pain with drugs or alcohol, but medicating *emotional* pain."

"Like the pain felt due to a wedding being called-off?"

"Exactly," Buchanan finger-pointed; "Do we know if Swenson has a drug or alcohol problem?"

"That information was not included in his Missing Persons Report," McCord replied, "but I imagine it's the kind of thing that would be addressed by the medical professionals who looked him over after the event."

"Yeah, I guess so."

"He has no record of DUIs or drug arrests," McCord noted, "so if he does have drug or alcohol issues he's managed to keep them under wraps."

"I take it that means we should make no mention of such a possibility in the report?"

"Why would we want to include that in the report?"

"You know... looking to impress the Captain by thinking outside the box – *'pondering possibilities'* as it were," Buchanan replied.

McCord shook his head, "You know as well as I that the report is a chronology of *facts*, not conjecture," he noted. "Documenting our thought process at the time, based on what we knew, *at the time*, which led to our specific actions, is the extent of conjecture that can go in a report."

"Can you repeat that in English?"

"We can document *why* we took a specific action, but that's pretty much it. For example: Why did we go in search of Swenson before the forty-eight-hour waiting period had elapsed?"

"Because his apartment manager called and said there was the smell of death coming from his apartment," replied Buchanan.

"Right. So we had a Missing Person, whom had been reported to be despondent, and now there were indications that he may be *missing* because he's *dead*."

"Got it," Buchanan replied. He looked at his computer screen, "That info is already in here."

"Yep," McCord grinned.

"What about including info that was in the News Tribune or the Register; those items that are identified as factual?"

"The report documents *our* words based on *our* actions, not some newspaper's account," McCord iterated. He paused in thought... "The Register?"

"Oh yeah," Buchanan replied, "there's a blurb here on their website that not only mentions the event, but that GHPD... us... posted some info on our social media page and thanked all of the responders and bystanders for their efforts."

"What the..." McCord started, "Do you have that up on your screen?"

"Yeah," Buchanan pointed, "right here."

McCord got up and moved over to view Buchanan's monitor.

"According to the Register," Buchanan continued, "our GHPD social media page got a number of shares, attracted hundreds of reactions, and dozens of comments."

"Have you seen the Department's post?"

"Not yet," Buchanan replied. He clicked on the associated GHPD media page link. "Check it out, they have the news station footage of you guys descending the bridge," he added and then nudged McCord, "You're a celebrity."

"Yeah... right," McCord shook his head and rolled his eyes.

The two Officers watched the video to the end.

"Wow, all the way through the reporter's interview with you," Buchanan commented.

"Yeah," McCord responded, "At least they didn't include the news anchor's update with Swenson's name."

"Good point."

"Hey, go back to the article from the Register."

Buchanan clicked back to the news article.

McCord read through the article and then stated, "And *there* it is," he shook his head.

"There *what* is?" replied Buchanan.

"It ends with *'the post received praise from a majority of the comments'.*"

"Yeah... so?"

"The magic word right there," McCord pointed at the screen, "Majority."

"Implying there are negative comments," Buchanan realized.

"Exactly," McCord exhaled.

"On the upside," replied Buchanan, "there's no way that Swenson follows our social media page."

"Let's hope you're right."

11

July 19th

Buzz-buzz-buzz-buzz continually echoed throughout the room. The swollen eyelids of a disheveled figure began to flutter. "What is that incessant buzzing?" he wondered. Reality began to sink in. His head slowly turned toward the repetitive annoyance. He squinted.

"Crap..." his raspy voice murmured as he looked at the clock.

He silenced the alarm, rolled back, and stared at the ceiling. He couldn't believe he had slept for the bulk of the past 24 hours, "Must have been the drugs the medics pumped me full of."

He looked at his cell phone; there were numerous voicemail messages. He hit 'Play':

"Hey Eric, it's Jeremy Whitworth from HR. I just wanted to tell you to take as much time off as you need. You've still got a couple days of sick leave on the books, plus some vacation days; and beyond that I'll just put you on LWOP, okay? Take care."

Swenson rolled his eyes, "Typical. Do your duty by making it sound like you're concerned, but all you're talking about is *me* using the time-off I *already* earned. And then once that's gone we'll let you have Leave Without Pay... whoop-dee-damn-doo."

"Yo Eric, it's Josh. Fuck that bitch... right?! Hey, when you're feeling better what say we throw down some suds at The Tides? Cheers to the single life, dude! Later."

Swenson's lower lip began to quiver; his eyes welled up with tears. His wound had been ripped open through the misguided attempt to relieve his pain by bashing the source of his heartbreak – an all-too-often testosterone-fueled exercise in poor judgment.

"Hi honey, it's your grandma. Someone from the police called and asked if you were here. I said NO and didn't know why they'd think you might be, but I promised to call them if you showed up. You know I don't have room here at the facility, especially with your Aunt Millie with all her problems showing up and staying overnight when she's not supposed to. She says it's not on purpose, but she sits and watches TV and then falls asleep on the couch and the next thing you know it's the next morning. The whole ordeal is causing my A-fib to act up. And you know I have that arthritis in my hip. And then there's my bunions on both feet so sometimes all I can wear are my mukluks because my shoes hurt too much. Millie got me one of those foot massager things but it hurts my feet more than the bunions... I don't know WHAT she was thinking. Okay, that was all... bye-bye."

Swenson could do nothing more than shake his head at his grandmother's rambling message. "Things never change," he said to himself aloud, "You hope for some level of concern, even maybe just a small hint, if nothing else. But nope... it always turns into a 'Woe is me' narrative about her maladies. I don't know whether to laugh... or cry."

"Hi Eric, it's me... umm... Heather. Just checking to make sure you're alright. Text me when you can; okay? Take care."

The tears welled-up in Swenson's eyes once again. His response wasn't solely due to hearing Heather's voice; it was both what she said, and what she *didn't* say, encapsulated in a single word... his name. No "Babe", no "Sweetie", no "Hon"; just "Eric"... the generic title bestowed upon someone whom could be nothing more than an acquaintance.

"Hey crybaby; you should've jumped!" a deep, husky voice rang out from Swenson's phone. He leapt from his bed to see the source of the message; but there was no name or number, merely the word "private". He could not believe what he had just heard, "Is this some kind of joke?!" he said aloud. His heart raced, his face became flushed with anger, his breaths turned rapid as his grief was overwhelmed by rage. He wiped the moisture from his eyes and then slammed his fist on

the bed, "Asshole!" he yelled at the phone. He replayed the message... increasing the volume... listening intently in the hopes that he might recognize the voice. It was to no avail.

His frustration and anger grew as he continually replayed the message. After the fifth attempt he stopped and stared at his phone. Silence overtook the room; a silence that was quickly drowned out by conversations within his own mind... a myriad of players, an array of emotions, no beginnings, ever-changing endings.

A thought came to the forefront. He jumped up, threw on some clothes, grabbed his cell phone, and headed out the door.

12

A haggard figure walked into the reception area of the Gig Harbor Police Station. He was unkempt, unshaven, bloodshot eyes, matted hair, and cloaked in rumpled clothes. He scanned the space and was surprised at the minimal size of the room: a closed door with an adjacent keypad to the immediate left, a small waiting area with three chairs to the right, a large metal box for depositing unused prescription meds at the far end beyond the seating area. To the left, directly across from the chairs, stood a counter fronted by a plexiglass window. Behind the glass stood two Department Administrative employees; one male, one female.

He stood at the entryway; appearing to be in somewhat of a stupor. The female behind the glass glanced over his way; she had a look of both curiosity and concern. She nudged her male counterpart and then ever-so-subtly head-nodded toward the man in the entryway. Her counterpart started to speak, but she beat him to it, "Can we help you?" she said to the man.

The man stepped up to the glass. "I need to speak to Officer McCord," he said.

"Do you have an appointment?" she asked.

"Tell him it's Eric Swenson; I'm sure he'll see me."

"Just a moment, please," she responded. She grabbed a phone, dialed three digits, and then stated, "Sergeant Patterson, I have a gentleman, Eric Swenson, here to see Officer McCord." She nodded, listened for several moments, and then spoke into the phone, "Thank you... I'll let him know."

She hung up the phone and turned to Swenson, "Officer McCord should be here momentarily."

"Thanks," Swenson replied and then shuffled over toward the seating area.

The door opened and Officer McCord stepped across the threshold. He immediately recognized Swenson and scanned him from head to toe; he was taken aback by the sight of the disheveled figure.

"Mister Swenson," said McCord as he extended his hand, "How are you doing?"

"I've been better," Swenson replied as he shook McCord's hand.

"What can I do for you?" McCord asked.

"I received a threatening phone call," Swenson replied, "Well… a threatening message," he clarified.

"Do you have it with you?"

"Yes," Swenson held up his cell phone.

McCord nodded toward the doorway, "Let's discuss it at my desk."

McCord and Swenson walked through the doorway, down a hall, and into an open office area. Buchanan looked up from his desk as McCord and Swenson approached.

"You remember Officer Buchanan," McCord said to Swenson.

"Yes," Swenson replied.

"Mister Swenson says he received a threatening message," McCord explained to Buchanan.

Swenson retrieved his cell phone and played the message for the Officers.

Buchanan looked somewhat surprised after hearing the message; McCord seemed to take it all in stride. "That was all?" McCord directed to Swenson, "He didn't say anything beyond calling you a name and saying that you should've jumped?"

"No," Swenson replied.

"Did you happen to recognize the voice?" Buchanan asked.

Swenson shook his head, "I listened to it a good half-dozen times, but nope… it doesn't sound like anyone I know."

"I hate to say it," McCord stated, "but the message does not specifically make any threats toward you."

Buchanan jumped in, "So the guy... the harasser... hasn't actually broken any laws."

"You can't trace the call, go talk to the guy, at least give him a warning about harassing me?" Swenson pleaded.

"Unfortunately there is no law against being a jerk," McCord replied, "Sorry."

"So, that's it?" Swenson responded, "This guy can just harass and bully someone?"

"If he actually makes a threat, then we can try to do something about it."

"TRY??" Swenson glared. "Just forget it!" he flailed his arms. "I wake up from a near-coma and all I have are a message from work telling me I can take Leave Without Pay, a buddy of mine's stupid dumbass message calling Heather a bitch, my grandmother's rambling message saying she doesn't want me to come around, Heather's generic message that might as well have been left to a coworker that she barely knew, this asshole who calls me a frickin' crybaby and says I should've jumped, and you guys say there's nothing you can do?! That's just terrific!"

Swenson turned around and began to walk away. "Maybe he's right... I should have jumped," he said as he walked out the door.

McCord looked at Buchanan. "And so it starts," he shook his head.

13

Officer McCord crossed his arms and exhaled; contemplating the exchange that Buchanan and he just had with Eric Swenson. "The seeds of the *worst case scenario* are starting to germinate... so it seems," he sighed.

"How's that?" Buchanan replied.

"Everyone who's supposed to be a part of Swenson's support system appears to be turning their backs on him."

Buchanan nodded, "Yeah, I see what you mean." He thought for a moment and added, "He looked awful... like he just crawled out from under a rock."

"No kidding," McCord replied. Something suddenly dawned on him. He looked toward Buchanan, "Why do you think his harasser called him a crybaby?"

"Maybe it was because of the article in the Tribune?" Buchanan replied.

"The Tribune?"

"Yeah; the article talked about the poem we found," Buchanan replied, "You know... with, what we thought might be, dried tear droplets."

"How could they have known about that?"

Buchanan had a look of guilt on his face. "I might have mentioned it," he lamented.

"What??" McCord glared, "When... when did that happen?"

"When you and Swenson were descending the bridge and the TV news crew was setting up," Buchanan explained, "a reporter from the Tribune walked over and asked me what was going on, so I gave him the rundown."

"Did the Captain give you permission to provide an official statement representing the Department?"

Buchanan looked beleaguered, "Well… no," he replied.

"Does she KNOW that you made a statement to a reporter that ended up in print?"

"I have no idea," Buchanan shrugged.

McCord responded with a 'What the hell?' gesture. Buchanan slumped down in his chair.

"Is that the article you were telling me about yesterday?"

"Yeah."

"Do you still have it?"

Buchanan opened his bottom desk drawer, extracted a newspaper, and handed it to McCord.

McCord silently read a few lines, stopped and glared at Buchanan, read a few more lines, scratched his head, and exhaled.

"You'll notice…" Buchanan pointed at the paper before McCord had a chance to provide his two-cents-worth, "…like I said before… I didn't mention Swenson by name."

"Which is a good thing," replied McCord, "but you've got the poems, the dead dog, and the somewhat-ominous text to the ex-fiancé in here," he said as he smacked the paper.

"Well they had to know why we showed up at his apartment, and why we were concerned about his well-being after visiting his ex," Buchanan explained. "And you see that I did *not* provide the details of the text, or give them his ex's name."

"Perhaps; but between this and the other news reports it's not going to take a mathematician to put two-and-two together."

Buchanan's mood turned solemn. The statuesque pride that he had been feeling in regard to the newspaper article just twenty-four hours ago had been reduced to rubble.

Just when Buchanan thought things couldn't get any worse, Sergeant Patterson approached – he had a newspaper in hand. *"Oh, great,"*

Buchanan thought to himself.

"Hey you two," Sergeant Patterson directed to McCord and Buchanan.

"Hey Sarge," replied Buchanan as he expected to get the *third degree* from the Sergeant.

"I just read the article in the Tribune," the Sergeant continued as he held up the newspaper, "Pretty good stuff."

Buchanan was surprised and immediately perked up, "Thanks."

"And I don't know how you guys came up with the possible tear droplets," added the Sergeant, "I don't think I would've noticed something like that."

"McCord's the one who caught that," replied Buchanan as he thumb-pointed at McCord.

"Ahh… that calibrated eyeball of yours, eh?" the Sergeant said to McCord.

McCord grinned and shrugged.

"Anyway," said the Sergeant, "Good job you two on this incident."

"Thanks," both McCord and Buchanan replied as the Sergeant walked out of the room.

Just as Buchanan had regained a smattering of his self-esteem an authoritative female voice rang out, "Officer Buchanan… a word."

Buchanan looked up to the sight of Captain Prescott's glare. It was a moment reminiscent of his youth, lacking only the use of his full name 'Nathan Thomas Buchanan!' and his Mother's accompanying hands-on-her-hips stance.

Captain Prescott turned around and vanished into her office. Buchanan, with a look of despair on his face, got up from his desk and followed suit.

14

McCord and Kayla grabbed a seat at a four-top table in The Tides Tavern; a popular, rustic establishment nestled upon the waters of the harbor. They sat next to each other; facing the entryway so that they could flag-down Buchanan and his date when they arrived.

It was the early evening of a warm July day; which meant a comfortable seventy-seven degrees, and a good two-to-three hours yet until sunset. McCord had traded-in his uniform for a pullover, a pair of slack-style shorts, and Sperry Top-Sider Boat Shoes. Kayla was clad in a skirt, tank top, and sandals. They were perusing the beverage menu.

"I'm trying to decide between a glass of white wine and a Cosmo," Kayla said to McCord.

"What about a Starburst?" McCord replied.

"Oh yeah, I forgot about those… they *are* quite tasty." She put down the menu and turned to McCord, "I suppose you're getting your usual?"

"Can never go wrong with a cold microbrew on a warm summer day," McCord smiled.

"There they are!" rang out from across the room. McCord looked up to see Buchanan and his date approaching.

Kayla turned to McCord and quietly stated, "Another date with Amanda… looks like things might be getting serious."

McCord gave Kayla a gentle 'Shush, they might hear you' jab.

"Hey guys," said Kayla to Buchanan and Amanda as they sat down.

Buchanan nodded; Amanda waved, "Nice to see you two again," she said.

"Likewise," replied Kayla.

McCord looked to Buchanan, "Sorry about busting your chops

earlier," he said.

"No problem," Buchanan replied, "I just chalked it up to another one of my *Life's Lessons Courtesy of Tyler McCord*." He scooted his chair closer to the table, "Besides; it was nothing compared to the Captain taking a bite out of my ass."

Amanda turned to Buchanan, then to McCord, and then back to Buchanan, "What are you guys talking about?"

"I made the mistake of providing the Tribune with a statement," Buchanan said, "without first clearing it through the Captain."

"The article about you two rescuing that guy off of the Narrows Bridge?"

"That's the one."

"I don't know why the Police Captain would be upset; I thought it was a nice article," Kayla jumped in, "It spoke very well of you two; and also showed genuine concern for the distraught gentleman."

"It wasn't so much the content," McCord explained, "Just that we didn't get clearance from either the Captain or the Public Affairs Officer."

"Oh; so it was a protocol thing."

"Yep," Buchanan replied. "And Ty's being kind when he says 'we', since it was really an 'I' thing," he said as he pointed at himself.

"The poor guy that almost jumped," said Amanda. "I saw him when they brought him in to the hospital... he looked to be in a pretty bad way... physically *and* emotionally."

McCord looked toward Amanda, "Did you happen to talk to him at all?"

"No," Amanda replied, "I wasn't one of the attending nurses."

"We talked to him this afternoon," Buchanan noted.

"Is he okay?" Amanda asked.

"That's open for debate," McCord replied.

"He looked like someone who had passed out behind a dumpster, woke up, and stumbled into the police station," Buchanan added.

"He stopped by the station?" Kayla chimed in.

"Yeah," McCord replied, "Some jerk-face left him a voicemail message saying that he should have jumped."

"Oh my Gosh," exclaimed Amanda, "How can people be so cruel?"

"Exactly," Buchanan sighed.

Kayla nudged McCord and whispered, "Just what you were worried about."

"Yep," McCord nodded.

"Did you go talk to the guy?" asked Amanda. "You know... the jerk-face?"

"His number was listed as 'private'," replied Buchanan.

"And he didn't actually make a threat, so we had no authority to attempt to trace the call," McCord added, "Plus it was likely untraceable anyway."

The four of them looked at each other; the grim subject matter had taken its toll. Fortunately, the server arrived to interrupt the dampened mood.

"Good evening," the server beamed, "Can I start you all off with some beverages?"

Once drinks had been ordered the conversation took a much more uplifting turn; "So..." Amanda directed to Kayla and McCord, "how did you two meet?"

Kayla responded with a grin, "Superficial Relationships dot-com."

McCord immediately broke into laughter. Buchanan glanced back and forth between McCord and Kayla, rendered a subdued laugh, and followed with a look of curious confusion.

"What??" Amanda responded to Kayla's statement.

McCord looked to Kayla with a wink and a grin, "I thought it was the website *Bro's and...*"

Kayla cut McCord off before he could finish, "Don't even go there," she pointed and glared.

McCord smiled and said to Kayla, "Okay, tell her how we *really* met."

Kayla responded back to McCord, "You go ahead."

"I noticed her," said McCord as he head-nodded toward Kayla, "multiple times at the monthly Art Walks here on the downtown waterfront."

"And I noticed him noticing me," grinned Kayla.

"Monthly Art Walks?" asked Amanda.

"Yeah, the first Saturday of the month about a half-dozen of the galleries here have featured artists, demonstrations, refreshments, sometimes musicians… you name it," replied McCord.

Amanda elbowed Buchanan, "How come you haven't taken me to one of these Art Walks?"

Buchanan grasped at a response, "Uhh… because I'm lacking culture?"

Amanda shook her head. She turned her focus back to Kayla and McCord, "So, you kept seeing each other at these Art Walks…" she prompted.

"But I never actually talked to her," McCord explained.

"Yeah… who would've figured *this* guy," Kayla nudged McCord, "would be the shy, quiet type?"

McCord shrugged and grinned. "And then one Saturday after the Art Walk I strolled over here and bellied-up to the bar to grab a bite," McCord continued. "I had just finished my meal and was enjoying my beer when a *certain woman*," McCord head-nodded at Kayla, "and her girlfriend grabbed the two barstools next to me."

"I immediately leaned over and said, '*Hey, it's the Art Walk Guy*,'" added Kayla. "And then he tried to introduce himself and could barely remember his own name," she giggled.

"Hey, I wasn't that bad," McCord retorted.

Kayla looked at Amanda and semi-whispered, "He was that bad."

"Anyway," McCord continued, "I told her that since I had seen her at so many of these events, that she must be some kind of art connoisseur."

Kayla jumped in, "Then I said that I have an *appreciation* for art, but can't lay claim to being a connoisseur… that I only started attending because I have a couple of friends who are artists who were showing their work in a couple of the galleries. And then I asked him *What about you?*"

"And I replied that I have an appreciation for the beauty of art in all its forms…" said McCord who then grinned, "Along with paintings, sculptures, and drawings," he winked.

"You didn't?" said Amanda.

"He did," Kayla responded. "And of course I replied *'Are you flirting with me?'*"

"And I said *'Busted'*," McCord replied.

"You guys are hilarious!" said Amanda.

"Oh, you haven't heard the coup de grace," noted McCord. "Tell 'em, babe," he said to Kayla.

Amanda and Buchanan looked at Kayla with anticipation.

"I told him I had noticed that gleaming smile he always sent my way, and it helped mold my first impression," said Kayla.

"What was your first impression?" asked Amanda.

Kayla elbowed McCord, "That he looked like someone who might want to buy me a drink."

"You said that?" replied Amanda.

"She did," responded McCord.

"Well, I had to do something to break the ice," Kayla explained.

"And obviously it worked," McCord nodded.

"And how about you two?" Kayla directed to Amanda and Buchanan.

"Superficial Relationships dot-com," Buchanan grinned.

"Oh, get out of here!" Amanda shoved Buchanan. "We met at the hospital."

"Nothing serious I hope?" replied Kayla.

"No," Buchanan said, "We first met when I broke my foot a year ago playing basketball, but we didn't really talk about anything except the circumstances around the break, my cast, how long I'd have to wear it, the limitations... all that stuff."

Amanda jumped in, "But later we crossed paths when they..." she nodded toward Buchanan and McCord, "came to the hospital to get statements from victims."

"Anyway," Buchanan added, "We got to talking, met for drinks one time, and here we are."

"So, a positive grew out of a negative," Kayla proclaimed.

"I hadn't thought of it that way," Amanda looked toward Buchanan, "but you're right."

"Life is full of surprises," said Buchanan.

"Ain't that the truth," noted McCord.

15

July 20th

Sergeant Patterson walked into the area of McCord and Buchanan's desks. "Hey you two," the Sergeant said, "a call just came in from a woman walking across the Narrows Bridge."

McCord and Buchanan perked up; Sergeant Patterson continued… "She heard a blood-curdling scream, looked over in that direction, and saw someone falling."

"Off the bridge?" said McCord.

"No; over near Lookout Point," replied the Sergeant. "And depending on the specific spot that they went over, we're talking about a hundred to hundred-fifty foot drop."

"Into the water?"

"That's something for you guys to try and figure out," said the Sergeant, "The person reportedly dropped out of sight, so we have no idea exactly where they landed."

"Crap; you don't think it's Eric Swenson do you?" said Buchanan.

McCord added to Buchanan's notion, "Yeah Sarge; Swenson was so frustrated and downtrodden yesterday after some asshole left him a harassing voicemail, that he stormed out of here mumbling that maybe he should have jumped after all?"

"No clue at this point; all the witness could see was someone falling," said the Sergeant. "We put in a call to the Coast Guard; but until they get there and launch a rescue attempt you two need to get over there pronto and see what, if anything, you can do. I've got EMTs on the way as well."

"Got it," replied McCord.

"The witness said she'll meet you at Lookout Point," said the Sergeant. "Be advised though, just so you know what to expect; according to CenCom she was pretty frantic... ranting and raving *"Oh my God, it can't be!"* ...and the like."

"Whoa!" replied Buchanan, "You got a name?"

The Sergeant looked at his memo pad, "Heather Kincaid."

"Holy crap!"

The Sergeant was caught off-guard, "You know her?"

"She's Eric Swenson's fiancé," replied Buchanan, "Well... ex-fiancé."

"The reason he was about to throw himself off the bridge," McCord clarified.

"Damn!" Sergeant Patterson responded.

"We're on it," said McCord as Buchanan and he bolted out of the Station.

- ❖ -

Lights flashing and siren blazing, McCord and Buchanan's cruiser transitioned from Grandview Street, to Pioneer Way / Wollochet Drive, to the highway onramp. Once through the onramp's hairpin turn, Buchanan gunned it as the Officers merged onto Highway 16.

Making their way toward Lookout Point, Buchanan relayed to McCord, "You got any thoughts on this?"

"Almost too many to make sense of at this point," McCord replied.

"What do you think about Heather Kincaid being the person who called it in?"

"To be honest, the first thing that came to mind was wondering if she was there with Swenson."

"And an argument or confrontation ensued, with him deciding to take the ultimate leap right in front of her?"

"It's possible," replied McCord, "although that would contradict the statement she made to CenCom."

"What do you mean?"

"She reported that she was on the bridge, too far away to see any details," McCord said. He pondered the situation and added, "But on the other hand, her exclamation *Oh my God, it can't be*" tends to imply she might know who it is."

"Which keeps bringing me back to Swenson," Buchanan noted.

"We'll know soon enough," stated McCord as they approached Lookout Point.

"What's the game-plan?"

"We're going to have to make it a rapid-fire, multi-pronged approach," replied McCord, "Talk to Heather along with any other witnesses, survey the scene and try to figure out where he or she went over... and if we can spot them; if so, then assess our ability to get to them, speak with them, and possibly get them to discuss the extent of their injuries."

"What if we can see them, and we yell out to them, but they're unresponsive?"

"If we're unable to get to them then all we can do is pass that info to the EMTs and the Coast Guard once they show up," replied McCord, "And provide whatever assistance they need from us."

"Got it."

The Officers wheeled into the parking lot at Lookout Point; they immediately noticed Heather standing near the railing that surrounds the entirety of the area.

McCord scanned the parking lot and commented, "No sign of Swenson's car," as the Officers rolled to a stop and scrambled out of their cruiser.

Heather flagged down the Officers. "Thank God you're here!" she said while almost hyperventilating; and then fired-off in rapid succession... "I don't know if it's Eric or not, but it could be. He just showed up out-of-the-blue while I was on the bridge and we got to talking. I guess he didn't like what I was saying because he got upset, turned back toward

Lookout Point, and stormed off. I was heading the other way... you know... toward Tacoma, so I just continued on my walk." She took a breath, "After several minutes something made me look back, and that's when I saw someone falling." She turned and pointed, "I think this might be where he went over." She gulped, "Oh my God!"

McCord held up his hand, "Wait here!" he directed to Heather.

McCord and Buchanan made a beeline to the railing. The Officers progressively trekked along the edge... stopping periodically for any signs indicating that a person might have gone over.

Buchanan turned back to Heather, "We're not seeing Mister Swenson's car in the lot here; so what makes you think he might be the person who went over the railing and down the cliff?"

"Sometimes he rides his bike," Heather replied.

"But then wouldn't his bike be around here somewhere?"

Heather was getting flustered, "I don't know!" she flailed her arms, "Maybe it went over the side with him?!"

That notion seemed extremely implausible to the Officers, but they decided not to question it.

"What about these other cars in the lot?" said Buchanan as he pointed, "Are any of them yours?"

"The blue and silver Outback," Heather responded.

Buchanan turned to McCord, "So the other two cars in the lot... one could be the vic's, the other could belong to a witness."

McCord nodded concurrence. "When we get a chance we'll call in the plate numbers; but the potential victim is our first priority." He began to walk the perimeter, "Look for evidence of shreds of clothing, flattened vegetation, broken branches that might indicate a person could've passed through there... anything that looks out of place."

"Got it," Buchanan replied. As he scanned the area he added, "Have you ever heard of anyone trying to jump from here?"

"Never," McCord replied. "This location has '*bust a thousand bones and quite possibly survive in excruciating pain*' written all over it. If you're looking for the 'sure thing instant death', this is not the place to achieve that objective."

Heather had quietly moved near the railing, but made sure to keep out of the way of the Officers. McCord glanced over and shook his head. He wanted to scold her for not following his directive, but decided there were more pressing matters at hand.

"Was anyone else here when you got here?" McCord relayed to Heather.

"No… not a soul," Heather replied.

"Damn," McCord said under his breath.

"How about when you saw the person falling?" added Buchanan, "Did you notice anyone over here at that time?"

"I wasn't focusing on this area," Heather replied, "I was trying to see where the person landed."

"What about as you approached?"

"I caught a brief glimpse of a small car, but that's about it."

"A small car?"

"Yeah; like maybe one of those Smart Car things."

"You didn't get a color, or see which way it headed?" added McCord.

"It was far away and the sun was in my eyes; all I got was mostly a silhouette," Heather replied, "And I didn't see which way they went; I only saw them leaving the parking area."

McCord looked west and then to Buchanan, "Well, the eastbound toll lanes and booths have cameras, so maybe we'll get lucky."

Buchanan nodded. He returned to his search and something caught his eye. "Hey Ty," he said as he pointed, "there's a rocky ledge down here with a relatively smooth patch surrounded by scattered debris."

McCord leaned over the railing where Buchanan was pointing, "Like someone might have slid through there," he noted.

"Exactly."

Heather ran over to the spot. "What… where?" she said as she gazed over the railing.

Buchanan pointed, "There."

McCord glared. "Please, ma'am," he said and then gestured for Heather to move back out of the way.

McCord scanned the grounds for a safe spot to climb over the railing. He spied an area where there were a few trees on the other side that, at the very least, he could latch onto if he slipped. He quickly made his way over to that spot and began to climb over the railing.

"What the hell are you doing?" said Buchanan.

McCord glanced back. "I'm going to get down to those trees in the hopes that I can see anything down below," he pointed.

"We don't need the Coast Guard to have to extricate TWO bodies out of here."

McCord essentially ignored Buchanan's statement and stepped foot on the other side of the railing. He took a couple of steps and immediately slipped on a bed of loose and moss-covered rocks. "Aww, shit!" he said as he slid several feet and slammed into one of the trees; wrapping his left arm around the trunk while simultaneously grabbing a large branch with his right hand.

McCord regained his footing and took a breath. "Well that sucked," he commented.

Buchanan gave McCord an 'I told you so' gesture.

McCord strategically repositioned himself, got a good grip on the tree branch with his left hand, and slowly shuffled to his right. He moved his head from one side to the other in search of an ideal vantage point. He crouched down. "Crap, I think I see something," he said, "But I can probably get a better bead on them from the next tree down."

"Are you frickin' kidding me?" replied Buchanan.

"Oh my God... is it Eric?" Heather yelled out.

"Can't tell from here," McCord replied.

The whoop-whoop-whoop of helicopter blades slicing through the air emanated from off in the distance, and they were getting louder.

"It sounds like the Coast Guard is here," said Buchanan, "Why don't you get the hell out of there and let them do their job?" he yelled out to McCord.

"Just give me a minute," replied McCord.

"Dammit," said Buchanan under his breath.

McCord worked his way around the tree, crouched down almost on his ass, and slid his way to the next tree. He stood up and returned his focus to the previous area of interest. "Yep, there's definitely someone down there… on a ledge… and they're not moving."

"Oh my God!" Heather buried her face in her hands.

"Hey down there, can you hear me?!" McCord yelled toward the person.

There was no verbal response; nor was there any movement.

"Helloooo… can you hear me?!" McCord repeated. "The Coast Guard is here; we'll be getting you out soon!"

As the helicopter got closer Buchanan began to alternate between waving his arms to get their attention, and pointing toward the approximate location of the victim.

The helicopter slowed to a hover. From McCord's vantage point the chopper pilot had located the individual.

"Hey Nate!" McCord yelled up to Buchanan. "Get on the horn with the Sergeant and let him know we're gonna need the Forensic Team out here; with mountaineering gear, including the ability to repel down the hillside."

The repetitive screams of a siren rang out… it was the EMT van.

McCord bear-crawled his way back up to the railing. He looked back toward the chopper; a rescuer was being lowered by cable to the scene. The rescuer dropped out of sight, followed shortly by an empty cable being raised back up to the chopper.

"Let's hope we're talking *rescue* and not *recovery*," McCord said to Buchanan.

"What do you mean?" Heather chimed in.

Both McCord and Buchanan remained silent. Heather connected the dots; a tear rolled down her cheek.

"What are you thinking in regard to the Forensics Team?" Buchanan asked McCord.

"I'm sure the Coast Guard will get photos of the vic and the immediate scene before they extricate him to the chopper," McCord replied, "but even if he survived he may not be able to tell us what happened."

"As to whether or not this was an accident?"

"Exactly," McCord nodded.

The EMT van pulled up next to McCord and Buchanan's cruiser; two EMTS emerged and headed toward the Officers.

"Officers," said one of the EMTs as he approached, "The Coast Guard chopper is lowering a rescue basket," he pointed toward the helicopter. "If the victim is still alive they're going to fly him to Saint Anthony's," he added, "unless his condition is so dire that the only option is to go directly to Harborview."

"Understood," replied McCord.

"We were only dispatched in the event we were able to get the victim back up here without the Coast Guard's involvement."

"Does that mean you've been in communication with the pilot?" asked Buchanan.

"That's correct."

"Any news on the victim's identification or condition?" said Buchanan.

"No word at this point."

A call came in to the EMT. "Yes, Sir," the EMT responded as he listened. "Understood… we'll stand by until you give us the all clear."

The EMT turned to the Officers and quietly said, "Bad news; the victim will be going directly to the Medical Examiner's Office in Tacoma."

McCord glanced over at Heather standing several feet away, and then turned back toward the EMT, "Any I.D. on him?"

"Caleb Rollins," the EMT replied. "But of course the Medical Examiner needs to make a positive identification, so that information should not be released."

"Of course," McCord replied. "Any idea on cause of death?" he added.

"Again... only the Medical Examiner can make that call; but he reportedly suffered massive head trauma, lacerations, broken bones, and dislocations... that's as much as I know."

"Got it; thanks."

McCord looked to Buchanan, "Well, it looks like it's up to the M.E. and forensics to figure out if we've got a tragic accident... or something sinister."

"Even if it's an accident we obviously need to figure out how it happened," Buchanan replied.

"True; although that would be the Accident Investigators area of responsibility at that point."

"So, I guess we're done here?"

"Almost," McCord replied, "I think we need to talk to Heather." He briefly glanced over at Heather; she looked like she'd been given a shot of Novocain and it was wearing off.

"To let her know that the I.D. on the vic is someone other than Swenson?" Buchanan asked.

"There's that," McCord replied. "Although God forbid it's not Swenson with someone else's I.D. on him," he pondered. "But also, we need to talk to her about their exchange on the bridge."

"Why is that?"

"To get an idea as to whether or not he is becoming a danger to himself," McCord thought for a moment, "Or worse... potentially to others."

16

She inserted her key into the deadbolt, turned it to unlatch the lock, extracted the key, then grasped and rotated the doorknob. She stopped; frozen in time, hand on the knob... the door still within its jamb. She quickly glanced to her left and then her right... anxiety had overtaken the moment. She took a deep breath, pushed the door open, and walked across the threshold. As she exhaled and placed her keys in a small tray on an end table she tried to hold back the tears; she was an emotional wreck. What had started out as an exhilarating trek along the Scott Pierson Trail on a warm summer day had been interrupted by the sudden appearance of Eric Swenson midway across the span of the Tacoma Narrows Bridge. A curious exchange that began with a tinge of unease had quickly turned tense, uncomfortable, borderline confrontational. She was trying to make sense of it all, but it was a seemingly impossible task.

She slowly made her way to the bedroom. She stopped at the nightstand and retrieved yesterday's memories... today's recollections... tomorrow's dreams. She grabbed a pen and began...

July 20th

Dear Diary,

How do you become strangers when you know someone so well? Or did you ever really know them? Perhaps it's a matter of "love is blind" until one day, unexpectedly, their true colors have shone through and you suddenly see the light. Was it all a ruse... a façade? You second guess yourself... the decisions you've made. You cry your eyes out to the point that you become numb – a mere shell of your former self. It all makes you wonder...

How is it that Eric happened to show up right when I was on the bridge? Was it simply a coincidence? Or has he been watching me? Was he looking to make another attempt to jump but wanted me to talk him out of it? Or worse, did he want me to witness him taking his own life; leaping to his death right there in front of me? But if that was the case then why did he keep looking at his watch? I was tempted to ask, but I wasn't sure if I wanted to hear the answer. And then, just as mysteriously as he showed up, he abruptly disappeared. It's all so confusing.

I feel bad about all of the taunting and bullying he says he's been receiving on social media. It isn't right, it isn't fair, it's heartbreaking. But what can I do? I tried telling him to delete his accounts, but he seems obsessed.

His calls, his texts, his 'suddenly showing up'... he's acting more and more like a stalker, and less and less like the man I was about to 'walk down the aisle' with. What do I make of it all? So many questions; no discernible answers. All I can think of is Raymond. I am overwhelmed with guilt.

17

"So the registered owner of the '99 Accord," said Buchanan, sitting at his desk after he and McCord had returned to the Station, "matches the I.D. found on the vic."

"Which gives us two pieces of circumstantial evidence as to the victim's identity," noted McCord. "I'm thinking we might want to at least make an initial look into this guy while we wait-out a positive I.D."

"It will be interesting to see what the M.E. and Forensics come up with."

"Yeah; it will let us know if we're diving into a murder case, or if we're simply providing input to the accident investigators," said McCord. "In either case, we may end being the ones who have to notify his next of kin."

"Ugh... I hate those calls."

"You and me both."

"What about that guy whose car was there, but said he didn't see anything?"

"Kovak?" McCord replied. "He willingly gave the Forensics Team a DNA sample, so that would tend to imply he wasn't involved; but we'll see what the lab and autopsy tell us."

"Autopsy?"

"If it shows the guy died from something *other* than the fall."

"Got it," Buchanan replied. He thought for a moment, "What do you think of Heather's exchange with Swenson?"

"To be honest, I'm struggling with that one," McCord replied, "From my perspective she wasn't totally forthcoming about it... like she was concerned, but didn't want to show it."

"I picked up on that as well," said Buchanan, "although I can't quite put my finger on it."

"My take is that she's realizing something is *off* about him, but she's trying to convince herself otherwise… essentially ignoring her intuition."

"That's a great way to put it," said Buchanan. "Notice how her *words* appeared to accept that nothing was out of the ordinary when Swenson *just so happened to show up* while she was walking across the bridge, but her *body language* told a completely different story."

"And how she mentioned his out-of-character behavior… his calls and texts… showing up at all hours at various locations," said McCord, "It was like she was purposely avoiding the word 'stalker', even though that's exactly what she was describing."

"Plus, her seeming to downplay his escalating mood swings," noted Buchanan, "From begging and pleading, to ranting and raving."

"You got that right," replied McCord. "Just one step away from being *threatening*," he took a breath, "If he hasn't gotten there already and Heather's keeping that from us."

"Are you implying that Heather's safety might be at risk?"

"Hard to say for sure, but if the source of his heartbreak becomes the source of his anger…" McCord's voice trailed off as he pondered the unthinkable.

"I see what you mean," Buchanan noted, "But until she files a complaint there's nothing we can do, right?"

"Well…" McCord considered the options, "we can attempt to make a preemptive strike of sorts."

"A preemptive strike?"

"Okay, perhaps that's a bit of an exaggeration," McCord stated, "But if we can identify some of Swenson's external stressors we might be able to make an assessment of his risk of getting pushed over the edge." McCord thought for a moment, "Uh… no pun intended."

"If I'm reading you correctly, you're talking about the concerns Heather shared with us?"

"Yep; not just his behavior, but what she told us about the negative comments he's allegedly receiving on social media."

"Along the lines of that *'you should have jumped'* voice mail message," Buchanan realized. He thought for a moment and added, "Does that mean trolling social media sites he might be a part of?"

"Not just those with which he is associated, but any that might have run, or shared, the news reports on 'the event'," McCord punctuated with air-quotes.

"So you're talking the local TV stations, newspapers, blogs…" replied Buchanan.

"And our own GHPD website," McCord responded, "Remember, they ran the story as well."

"Should we also be tracking his movements?"

"We don't have probable cause for such an action," McCord replied. "Even though he appears to be having difficulty coming to grips with the breakup he has no history of violence toward others, only that of putting his own life in jeopardy."

"So, we limit our investigation to those things that could be dragging him toward the whirlpool, and hopefully intervene if he appears to be spiraling into the abyss?"

"Until a directive from a pay grade above ours dictates otherwise," replied McCord, "you're exactly right."

18

His breaths ran rapid as he rolled The Silver Specter down the hallway, took a left, then another left into the laundry room. His heart raced; his hands shook… reliving the events of the afternoon. Rejection is a terrible thing; it can drive you to become a version of yourself that you never knew existed… to taking actions you never would have imagined.

As he placed the bicycle on hooks at the far end of the laundry room he accidentally bumped the front tire – it spun like a roulette wheel. "Red or black… odd or even," he said aloud while it spun. "And the answer *is*…? None of the above," he responded as the wheel rolled to a stop. "Better cash-in your chips before…" he stopped himself. "Hmm… poor choice of words," he stated after considering where his comment was going.

He removed his riding gloves and draped them over The Silver Specter's crossbar. He turned back around and caught the sight of Mister Brewster's former residence. The doggie bed was still there, but it was now nothing more than a shrine to '*what was*': his favorite chew toy, favorite stuffed dinosaur, favorite blanket. He stopped and stared at the emptiness, reminiscing about days gone by. The loss of one's loyal companion would normally invoke heartache… sadness… reflection; but when added to a life already unraveling an entirely different range of emotions had taken hold. He clenched his fists and screamed at the top of his lungs, "AAAHHH!!" …until there was no more air within them.

He dropped to his knees, almost gasping as he attempted to recover his oxygen. His breaths grew large and deep as he knelt in, what was otherwise, the silence of loneliness. He wiped the spittle from his chin; and the moisture from his eyes. Bracing himself against the washing machine he slowly stood and began a morose trek to the kitchen.

He opened the refrigerator door, grabbed a Pale Ale, and placed it on the counter while the door swung shut. He extracted a bottle opener from a drawer, popped the top of the beer bottle, and replaced the opener. He took a swig and then wiped his mouth with his forearm. He opened the freezer door and extracted a rice bowl. He nudged the door shut and removed his meal from the carton. Pulling up the edge of the cellophane to break the seal and allow a vent path he smiled at his chosen alternative to the 'punch holes in the cellophane' directive from the instructions. He placed the rice bowl in the microwave, punched in the requisite number of minutes, and hit 'start'. He took another swig of beer.

While his meal was rotating on the turntable he made his way to what had become his nemesis... his computer; or more specifically, his obsession with all things related to the event a few days prior. It had started with the high he felt due to the coverage and associated positive comments in regard thereof; he had become something of a celebrity. But in this day and age the unfortunate truth is that with adoration comes ridicule, and seeking out that initial high can be an ill-fated endeavor. The notion of obsessive behavior was not completely lost on him; he logged on and proclaimed aloud, "Like a junkie needs his dealer; like a gambler needs... well... his dealer." He grinned at the irony – the same name with entirely different, yet essentially the same, connotation. Alas, the grin would be fleeting.

He realized that his life was being overtaken by the need to follow associated news feeds and social media, but he was losing his ability to reason with the compulsion. What he was failing to recognize was that the impact of the ridicule... the bullying... the taunting... had assumed control. The search for compliments, for understanding, for adoration, had become sporadic at best, if not almost non-existent. Seeking out the negativity that was directed his way was now stoking the embers; the more that they drew his ire, the more 'alive' he felt.

But today was different – his emotions were contradictory... stoked equally by grief, and by rage. Passion can manifest itself in many forms. Where would it all lead?

The *ding* of the microwave rang out.

19

July 21st

"Sheesh," Officer Buchanan exhaled as he stared at his computer screen.

McCord looked over toward Buchanan, "Computer kicking your butt? Got the 'blue screen of death'?"

"Nah," replied Buchanan, "I started to compile a list of all the negative, or at least questionable, comments about Swenson on the various news feeds and such, and it's turning into a nightmare."

"Are you talking content; or quantity?"

"Both," said Buchanan. "If I try to capture each and every one of them I'll be here until next Tuesday."

"There are that many insensitive jerks out there?"

"I'm afraid so," Buchanan lamented.

"Unbelievable," McCord shook his head. An option came to mind, "Instead of trying to capture all of them; how about just identifying the source along with the date and time of the comment?"

"I like the way you think," Buchanan pointed at McCord.

McCord pondered for a moment, "Did Swenson happen to respond to any of those comments?"

"A number of people stood up for him; fortunately," Buchanan replied, "A bit of *bashing back at the bashers* as it were, but I didn't see anything that looked like it was from Swenson."

"Hard to believe a guy his age wouldn't potentially be a social media junkie; but hey, perhaps we got lucky."

"Or he's able to let the negativity slide off of him like teflon," countered

Buchanan.

McCord gave Buchanan the stink-eye, "You're kidding, right? He had an *absolute fit* from a single 'you should have jumped' voicemail message."

"Yeah," Buchanan nodded, "I guess I had a bit of a brain freeze on that one."

"That would be an understatement," McCord grinned.

"What about on your end?" Buchanan started, "Anything interesting on the guy that took the tumble?"

"From what I'm finding," McCord responded, "Caleb Rollins is not exactly a candidate for 'Citizen of the Year'."

"What's the deal on him?"

"Not that I'm implying that people will be celebrating his demise," McCord explained, "but he's gotten into plenty of scrapes regarding harassment, disturbing the peace, making threats, drunk and disorderly..."

"Out of curiosity, are there any arrests for assault?"

"Surprisingly... No."

"He's one of those *all talk and no action* kind of bullies some of us had to put up with in grade school and junior high?"

"So it seems," McCord replied. "And wow does he ever rant and rave on his social media page. You know... the type who has an opinion about almost everything... ninety percent of which is negative."

"Where it seems all they want to do is whine and complain about stuff? Or have some need to disparage others?"

"Yep."

Buchanan shook his head, "I don't get the whole 'rant' thing at all."

"I'm with you on that," McCord replied. "If you have an opinion that you feel an overwhelming need to share, why wouldn't you make a well-informed, fact-driven, calm and rational comment? Ranting and raving simply makes it look like you've *gone off the deep end*; in which case you could completely undermine a *legitimate* point of view because of your irrational behavior. Ridiculous!"

"I concur," said Buchanan. "And along those lines; is there any verbal sparring in there?"

"Yeah, but nothing that says 'let's meet up behind the grandstand and settle this once and for all'," McCord replied.

"Hey McCord... Buchanan," said Sergeant Patterson as he walked in the room while periodically glancing over a sheet of paper, "A preliminary report from the Medical Examiner just came in on Caleb Rollins."

McCord held out his hand; the Sergeant handed him the report. "Looks like you guys are off the hook," the Sergeant replied as he walked away.

"What's it say?" Buchanan directed to McCord.

"Rollins died of a cerebral contusion... blunt force trauma to the skull," McCord read aloud.

"What about all that other stuff the EMT mentioned," Buchanan replied, "the lacerations, broken bones, and dislocations?"

"Those are all in here as well; just not identified as the C.O.D."

"Bottom line?"

"The injuries are consistent with a fall," McCord read.

"I take it that means the cause of death has been ruled an accident?"

"That's the preliminary ruling," said McCord. He turned to face Buchanan, "Apparently forensics didn't find anything conclusive that would dictate otherwise."

"Hence our being *off the hook* as the Sergeant stated."

"I reckon so," replied McCord as he placed the report on his desk.

20

"Ugh... next-of-kin notifications... one of my least favorite aspects of the job," Buchanan stated as McCord and he drove toward the home of Caleb Rollins' mother.

"You and me both," McCord stated.

"What's the story on his next of kin?"

McCord looked at his memo pad, "Isabelle Rollins, age fifty-seven; the mother of Caleb," he replied. "It's also Caleb's residence."

"He's thirty-four and still lives with... well, lived with... his mother?"

"According to County Records."

McCord and Buchanan pulled up to the curb of the Rollins residence. They exited their cruiser, trekked along the home's pathway, stepped onto the landing, and rang the doorbell.

A woman, appearing to be beyond her years, opened the door. She was wearing a muumuu, grey hair all ratted like Grandmamma from the Addams Family, discolored fingertips, reeked of nicotine, and was barefoot... her toenails overly-long such that they curled over her toes – looking to be in drastic need of an anti-fungal medication.

The Officers were taken aback by the sight, but made sure to maintain their composure. "Mrs. Rollins?" McCord inquired of the woman.

"It's MISS," Mrs. Rollins replied, "That no-good husband of mine walked out on me and Caleb when the boy was just a baby; haven't heard from that worthless-excuse-for-a-father in over thirty years. You call that a father? I don't call that a father. I've been both mother and father to that boy ever since."

"Yes, ma'am," McCord replied, "We're actually here about your son."

"What has my shit-for-brains son gotten himself into this time?" Mrs.

Rollins responded.

Mrs. Rollins' response took McCord by surprise; he had never heard a mother provide such a descriptor of her son before. He glanced over at Buchanan; whom appeared to have the same reaction.

"Ummm…" McCord stumbled as he attempted to reply to Mrs. Rollins, "Are you familiar with the gentleman who took a fall off of Lookout Point?"

Mrs. Rollins became irate and defensive, "My boy may have a bit of a temper, but there is no way he was involved in that!"

"I'm sorry to say ma'am, but your son is the victim."

Mrs. Rollins stood in stunned silence. The moment was brief; she suddenly erupted in anger, "Who did this to him?! Are they under arrest?! I want them locked up for life!"

Buchanan jumped in, "I'm sorry ma'am, but all evidence points to an unfortunate accident."

"An accident?"

"I'm afraid so."

"At Lookout Point?"

"That's correct."

"Why would he be at Lookout Point?" Mrs. Rollins demanded.

"That's what we were hoping you might help us with," said McCord.

"I have no idea," Mrs. Rollins replied. "How did it happen?"

"It appears that, for some reason, he climbed over the railing that surrounds the parking area," explained McCord, "and then he slipped and fell… landing on a ledge down near the bottom of the hillside."

"That makes no sense!" Mrs. Rollins replied, placing her hands on her hips.

"Why is that?" asked Buchanan.

"He was afraid of heights," Mrs. Rollins replied, "There's no way he would have put himself in danger by climbing over the railing near the edge of a cliff!"

"Unfortunately, ma'am; there doesn't appear to be any other

explanation," said McCord.

"Don't give me that nonsense; you boys get your heads out of your asses and find out who did this!"

"Yes ma'am," McCord replied and handed Mrs. Rollins his card, "Please give us a call if you have any further questions, or any information to provide."

Mrs. Rollins stood in the doorway and stared at McCord's card. The Officers turned around and walked back to their cruiser. As they pulled away from the curb McCord, riding shotgun, looked back toward the house – Mrs. Rollins just stood there, glancing back and forth between McCord's business card and the cruiser as the Officers drove out of sight.

"Well that wasn't what I expected," McCord relayed to Buchanan.

"What part are you talking about?" replied Buchanan.

"All of it."

"Yeah," Buchanan exhaled.

– ❊ –

"How did Mrs. Rollins takes the news?" Sergeant Patterson inquired of McCord and Buchanan as they walked into the police station.

"I think we can sum it up in one word," replied McCord, "Denial."

The Sergeant was confused, "Denial? That's not an uncommon response for a suicide; but for an accident?"

"Yep," McCord shrugged. "So be advised that she might begin hounding the station for answers."

"For answers??" replied the Sergeant. "Well, write it up and I'll deal with…" he shook his head, "with *whatever*."

21

July 22nd

"Ready to roll?" McCord said to Kayla as they were all suited-up in preparation for venturing down the road on their bicycles.

"Was that a pun?" Kayla replied.

"Sorta," McCord grinned.

Kayla shook her head, "Let's ride," she smiled as she climbed aboard her bike and started down the Scott Pierson Trail. McCord followed suit.

"What a perfect day to be free-wheelin'," commented McCord as he caught up to Kayla.

"A Sunday 'ride' beats a Sunday 'drive' any day," Kayla proclaimed.

"I don't know..." McCord responded, "It's pretty hard to beat a drive along the North Cascades Highway this time of year."

"Okay, you've got me there," Kayla acknowledged, "But that's not a Sunday drive... more like a weekend excursion."

"Good point," McCord replied, "And you know what we always say when we get to Winthrop?"

"What's that?"

"Giddy up!" McCord grinned as he kicked-it-up a notch; leaving Kayla in a cloud of dust.

"You jerk!" Kayla yelled and kicked-it-up herself in pursuit.

McCord was smiling like a mischievous schoolboy when Kayla caught up to him.

Kayla looked over at McCord, "You'd better watch out, what goes around comes around."

McCord shrugged with an accompanying *'who me?'* grin.

"Don't try to use those puppy dog eyes on me, Buster."

After a few moments of silence Kayla stopped pedaling and began to coast. McCord followed her lead… they were approaching the bridge. Kayla rolled to a stop; McCord hit the brakes.

"What's up, babe?" McCord asked.

Kayla looked up, "I can't believe you were on the top of that tower."

"Looking up at it now I can't believe it either," McCord replied, "I don't know what I was thinking."

"You were thinking someone needed help before it was too late."

"Yeah," McCord exhaled, "And I'm afraid that story is still being written."

Just as they were about to recommence their ride McCord noticed someone with their dog walking toward them, and they looked familiar. The person was oblivious to McCord and Kayla, and almost bumped into them as they approached.

"Ms. Kincaid?" McCord called out to the woman.

Heather was startled; she didn't recognize McCord at first… his being out of uniform and wearing a bicycle helmet.

"Oh," Heather stated, "Officer McCord."

"This is my wife, Kayla," said McCord as he made introductions. "Kayla, this is Ms. Kincaid."

Heather reached out to shake hands with Kayla, "Please, call me Heather," she said.

"Nice to meet you," Kayla replied.

McCord crouched down, "And who do we have here?" he said as he petted the dog.

"This is Cassie," Heather replied.

"Yours?" said McCord.

"My parents."

"She's a beauty," Kayla chimed in.

"Yeah, she's about as awesome as they get," Heather replied, "Thanks."

"We're biking the trail," McCord stated as he stood back up, "and then I think we're gonna make a detour down to Titlow Park," he looked over to Kayla.

Kayla nodded concurrence with McCord's statement.

"That sounds fun," Heather stated.

"I'm guessing you must enjoy walking the trail?" McCord said to Heather.

"It used to be one of my favorite places to get lost in my thoughts and enjoy the view on a nice day," Heather replied, "But after the whole thing with Eric it is losing its luster."

"I'm sorry to hear that," Kayla responded to Heather's comment.

"Yeah," Heather sighed. "Thankfully I have Cassie here," she petted the dog, "to brighten up my walk and help me forget about such things."

"I completely understand," McCord replied.

The three of them looked at each other as they all appeared to be somewhat at a loss for words.

"Well..." McCord broke the silence, "I guess we should get back on the road here."

"Oh, of course," Heather responded.

"Nice to have met you," Kayla said to Heather.

"Me too," Heather replied.

McCord reached down and petted the dog one more time, "Goodbye Cassie."

The three of them waved. Heather and Cassie began to resume their trek when Heather suddenly stopped and turned around as McCord was getting back on his bike, "Umm... Officer?" Heather called out.

McCord stopped in his tracks. "Ma'am?" he inquired.

"Can I...?" Heather stammered, "Can I talk to you about something?"

McCord looked to Kayla, who gave him a 'talk to her' nod; he then looked back to Heather, "Of course," he said.

"Things with Eric are getting worse, and it has me worried," Heather stated.

"The types of things you were mentioning a couple of days ago?"

"Yes," Heather dropped her head, "I hate to admit it, but I held back about how bad it has gotten."

"I had suspected as much," McCord replied, "Have you filed a report?"

"I'm hoping things don't have to get to that," Heather responded, "I'm afraid he is close to the breaking point."

"I understand," McCord replied. "Officer Buchanan and I will stop by and have a talk with him when we're out on patrol."

"Thank you."

"You're welcome."

Heather turned and resumed her trek with Cassie; the dog taking the lead.

Kayla brushed McCord's face, "You okay, Hon?" she asked.

"I'm good... thanks." McCord paused in thought, "Hey, since we're here, do you mind if we make a quick detour over to Lookout Point before we head to the park?"

"Not at all," replied Kayla as she hopped back onto her bike.

McCord hopped onto his bike as well and the two of them made the quick two-minute ride over to Lookout Point – stopping near the spot where McCord had previously investigated.

"What's on your mind, babe?" said Kayla as McCord started eyeballing a certain area.

"Something that Caleb Rollins' mother said yesterday," McCord responded as he started looking around near the area where Rollins tumbled to his death.

"What's that?"

"She said her son was afraid of heights," McCord looked... and crouched... and rubbed his palm along the handrail, "So it made no sense for him to put his life at risk either leaning against, or climbing over, a rail whose next step was an almost-vertical drop of a hundred feet or more."

"If this is where he fell," Kayla stated, "How did he get from here," she pointed at the railing, "to way down there?"

"Hmm…" McCord pondered, "Interesting…"

22

Rap-rap-rap Officer McCord knocked on the door of Eric Swenson's apartment – Officer Buchanan at McCord's side.

The Officers heard faint footsteps approaching from the other side of the door, followed by a few seconds of silence. The footsteps recommenced, and then faded away.

The Officers looked at each other; Buchanan issuing a 'What the hell?' gesture. McCord yelled out, "Eric Swenson; Officers McCord and Buchanan, can we have a few moments of your time?"

No response.

"Mister Swenson!" McCord reiterated.

A muffled "Just a minute" was heard in response.

"What do you think is going on in there?" Buchanan quietly asked McCord.

"Just got out of the shower and is throwing on some clothes?"

"Maybe he's got a woman with him?"

"We'll have major egg on our faces if it happens to be Heather."

"Unless she's here under a scenario that I don't want to imagine," Buchanan grimaced.

"Crap," McCord responded, "I hadn't even considered such a possibility."

The Officers suddenly found themselves in a heightened state of caution.

The sound of footsteps approaching the door once again became audible. Swenson opened the door – he was all beat to hell... multiple bruises, scratches, and his hands all scraped up. He was wearing a rugby outfit that read *Gig Harbor RFC*.

The Officers scanned Swenson from head to toe. "What happened?" McCord inquired of Swenson.

"Rugby," Swenson replied as he thumb-pointed at his outfit. "What can I do for you gentlemen?" he added.

"We're talking to persons who were on or near the Narrows Bridge a couple of days ago in the early afternoon," McCord replied.

"What makes you think I was there?"

"Heather Kincaid called 9-1-1 saying that she saw someone falling," McCord explained. "We were dispatched to investigate, and she told us why she was there, and what she had seen."

"And she told you that I was there?"

"She said she ran into you on the bridge," Buchanan chimed in.

"Well, as you can see," Swenson spread his arms wide, "I am just fine... no fall, no swan dive."

"There's more to it than that," said McCord.

Swenson was getting flustered, "What, I can't take a stroll across the bridge without you guys thinking I'm there to climb the suspension cables?!"

"We aren't here in regard to your being on the bridge," McCord explained, "We're here because you were in the general vicinity, and approximate time, that a gentleman took a fatal fall near Lookout Point."

Buchanan chimed in, "So we're talking to anyone who might have seen something."

"Didn't see a thing," Swenson replied.

"Did you happen to know him?"

"Know who?"

"The gentleman who took the tumble," stated McCord.

"Beats me," Swenson replied, "What's his name?"

"Caleb Rollins."

"Doesn't ring a bell," Swenson shook his head.

"You didn't see him at all; or someone else nearby?"

"Like I said… didn't see a thing."

McCord jotted in his memo pad.

"Is that all?" asked Swenson.

"As a matter of fact… not quite."

Swenson had grown perturbed, "NOW what?"

"Heather continues to be concerned about your well-being," McCord replied.

"How do you mean?"

"She said you still seem rather troubled, haven't been back to work… she's worried."

Swenson crossed his arms.

"She also said you're calling and texting a lot, showing up at all hours of the day and night," McCord stated, "And showing up at places that seem to be more than merely a coincidence."

This piece of news drew Swenson's ire, "What… she's filing a restraining order against me?!"

"She doesn't want it to get to that; she just wants some private time… doesn't want to be looking over her shoulder when she goes out… doesn't want to feel a sense of angst when there's a knock on the door… doesn't want to feel uneasy every time her cell phone rings," McCord replied. "This has all been difficult on her."

Swenson exploded, "Difficult on HER?!!"

The Officers were startled; they both gave Swenson a stern glare.

Swenson realized he was treading on thin ice. He exhaled and responded, "Fine!"

The three men stood in uncomfortable silence.

"Can I go now?" Swenson said as he grasped the doorknob.

"Of course," McCord replied, "Thanks for your time."

Swenson shook his head and shut the door.

As the Officers were walking away Buchanan relayed to McCord, "I had no idea you were going to ask him about what he might have seen… you know… Rollins."

"That was part smokescreen, part actual interest," McCord replied.

"How's that?"

"I wanted the questions about Heather to appear to be more of an afterthought... putting a little less heat on her."

"You're a sneaky bastard, you know that?" stated Buchanan.

"Not just me," McCord replied. "Once I started down the path about Rollins, did you notice how you jumped in like you had rehearsed the script? That was one hell of an ad-lib."

"Apparently I've learned a few tricks from the master," Buchanan grinned.

When the Officers got to their cruiser McCord stopped and pulled out his cell phone, "Hang on a sec," he said to Buchanan. He punched in a phone number and waited for a response.

"Hello?" emanated through the phone.

"Ms. Kincaid, this is Officer McCord."

"What can I do for you?" Heather replied.

"Where are you right now?" asked McCord, "If you don't mind me asking."

"I'm at home," Heather responded, "Why?"

McCord sighed relief, "I simply wanted to let you know that Officer Buchanan and I just had a nice chat with Mister Swenson."

"I greatly appreciate that," Heather replied, "Thank you."

"You're welcome."

Kitsap Sentinel – July 23rd

NORTH KITSAP - A body was discovered early this morning in a marsh that spans several acres near Stottlemeyer and NE Iverson Roads in unincorporated Kitsap County, midway between Poulsbo and Kingston. Although the name of the victim has not been released pending notification of next of kin, Kitsap County Sheriff's Department spokesperson Sergeant Regina Carlson stated that the victim was a 2010 graduate of Hood Canal High School. Sergeant Carlson also stated that they are treating the cause of death as a possible homicide. Details concerning the manner of death are not being released at this time. Ironically, it was twenty-five years ago yesterday that the body of Justin Coleman was discovered in this exact location. A Purple Heart recipient, Justin was one of the tragedies of the Gulf War that are all too often forgotten or dismissed; he survived his time in Kuwait and Iraq, but fell prey to the demons the war had brought him. He died of a self-inflicted gunshot wound just a few days shy of his twenty-third birthday. A remembrance of Justin's life was held at the historic St. Paul's Church in Port Gamble at 7pm Sunday evening; over one hundred mourners and honored guests from local military bases were in attendance.

23

July 23rd

"Hey, were you able to make it to that memorial service last night?" Buchanan relayed to McCord as he arrived for duty at the police station.

"Technically, it was more of a remembrance since the guy passed away twenty-five years ago," McCord replied. "But yes; it was a nice service."

"Was that the one that was mentioned in the paper?"

"Beats me," shrugged McCord, "I haven't read the paper."

"The Kitsap Sentinel mentioned a service in Port Gamble for a guy who served in The Gulf War."

"The Sentinel? Do you read every paper in the Kitsap and Olympic Peninsulas, or what?"

"I like to keep abreast of what's happening in our extended area."

"Well, you are correct; it was a service for Justin Coleman," McCord replied. "I never knew him, but he was my uncle's best friend from the time they were kids up through high school."

"Are you aware of the eerie coincidence regarding the location his body was found?"

McCord was confused, "What are you talking about?"

"The bit about the memorial service was an 'Oh by the way piece of irony' regarding the primary focus of the article."

McCord glared, "How about you just cut to the chase?"

"A body was found this morning in the exact same spot that Justin Coleman committed suicide twenty-five years ago."

"Whoa; what else do we know?"

"Not much," Buchanan replied, "No name... although the person is said to be a 2010 graduate of Hood Canal High School; and no cause of death except that the Kitsap County Sheriff's Department is treating it as a potential homicide."

McCord and Buchanan's conversation was interrupted by the appearance of Captain Prescott. "It sounds like you two are discussing Kitsap County's new homicide case," the Captain stated.

"Only what I read in the paper," Buchanan replied.

"Keep this under wraps for the time being, but here's what they know right now," said the Captain, "Male, preliminarily identified as Jared Paget, age twenty-six, born and raised in North Kitsap. Cause of death – blunt force trauma to the skull."

"Do we know the murder weapon?" asked McCord.

"There was the mandible from a large animal... best guess bovine or equine... near the scene, covered in blood," replied the Captain, "but forensics has yet to confirm it as the weapon."

"What do you think, Cap?" said McCord, "Is the killer making some kind of a statement? Or was it a weapon of opportunity?"

"There are numerous ranches in the area... horses, cows, even llamas," stated the Captain, "so it certainly appears we're talking weapon of opportunity."

"That would tend to imply the murder was not premeditated," McCord stated, "and, instead, an argument got heated, turned into an altercation, and ended in murder."

"Which would also imply that the victim knew his killer," Buchanan chimed in.

"Kitsap County law enforcement is looking at it through a similar lens," the Captain stated.

"Are they requesting our assistance on this?" asked McCord.

"Not at this time; they are merely sharing information," replied the Captain, "However; depending on evidence gathered from the victim and the scene, further leads, etcetera, you never know when a case might cross jurisdictional boundaries."

"Understood," McCord responded.

Captain Prescott exited the space. Buchanan noticed that McCord seemed to be in deep contemplation. "Hey Ty," Buchanan interrupted McCord's train of thought, "Something on your mind about the case in Kitsap?"

McCord snapped back to reality, "Nah; the oddities of *that* case merely jogged my memory about a couple of the oddities from yesterday's visit with Swenson."

"What's that?"

"His actions and appearance," replied McCord. "Starting with the fact that he obviously walked up to the door, spied us through the peephole, and then went back to take care of 'who knows what' before he opened the door to talk to us."

"Hiding something, perhaps?" said Buchanan.

"Possibly," McCord sighed, "Although we have no probable cause to execute a search at this time, unfortunately."

"And if he was hiding something, he likely destroyed or discarded it as soon as we left."

"I concur," McCord replied, "However, his behavior could be tied to his *appearance*."

"His being all beat to hell?"

"That plus his outfit."

"Okay, you've lost me on that one," Buchanan replied.

"His outfit, although covered in dirt and grass stains, was completely dry," said McCord, "There's no way he had just been in a scrum."

"Whoa," Buchanan nodded, "I didn't even notice that contradiction."

"And check this out," McCord pointed to his computer screen, "Gig Harbor RFC's schedule... the match did NOT occur yesterday; it was the day before – Saturday."

"So the bastard tried to con us," Buchanan noted very matter-of-factly.

"Yep."

"What do you think was his reason for the smokescreen?" said Buchanan, "What's he trying to hide?"

"Your guess is as good as mine, but we need to take a closer look at this guy."

Buchanan nodded. He noticed that McCord still seemed to be staring off into space. "Something else on your mind?" he said.

"Yeah," McCord replied, "Something that Kayla noted when we were out at Lookout Point near the spot where Rollins fell."

"What's that?"

"We looked at the distance between the railing, and where Rollins took the tumble," McCord replied, "and she made a rather astute observation."

"Yeah?"

"She wondered how Rollins got from 'here'," McCord mimicked, "to 'there'."

"Maybe forensics and the M.E. will address that detail; or speculation in regard thereof," replied Buchanan, "In their final report?"

"Let's hope."

24

July 23rd

Dear Diary,

I talked to Miranda today. I told her about Eric and me. I had been holding off, but since her and Colby's Rehearsal Dinner is just a few days away I needed to let her know that Eric wouldn't be there for it. I didn't want to share too much; after all, she should be excited about the happiest day of her life coming up, and not worrying about me. But of course, what do best friends do? They ask questions when they are concerned about you. She got almost frantic when I told her about Eric's strange behavior; luckily I was able to calm her fears when I told her that Officers McCord and Buchanan went and talked to him. After I got her to calm down I decided that I would not tell her about the poem I found in my purse the other day. I don't know how Eric snuck it into my purse. Has he been following me and put it there when I got up for something and left it unattended? But I am never without my purse, so that wouldn't make sense. Did he sneak into my house and put it there? If so, then how did he do that while I was home? Did he sneak in late at night while I was asleep? Or maybe while I was in the shower? I'm totally creeped-out just thinking about it. Wait... something just dawned on me: I don't take my purse with me when I go jogging; maybe he got in the house while I was out pounding the pavement? Maybe that's why he suddenly took off while we were talking on the bridge; that he had to get back here and plant the note before I got home? This whole thing is such a mess. I haven't told the Officers yet about the note. I think I should.

25

July 24th

"Check this out," Buchanan said to McCord, "I think I might have come up with a reason for Swenson's smokescreen."

"Yeah?" McCord perked up.

"Guess where he and his grandmother lived before she moved to Northern California and left him here to fend for himself?"

"I'm assuming someplace noteworthy based on the inflection in your voice."

"You got that right; it was the same neighborhood as Caleb Rollins."

"Implying that Swenson was feigning ignorance when we asked if he knew Rollins," McCord nodded.

"Exactly!"

"Whoa, that is quite the coincidence," McCord pondered. "But Rollins is a good eight or nine years older than Swenson. When I was a kid I paid little or no attention to some dude eight or nine years older than me."

"What if it was your best friend's older brother?"

"Well in that case… sure," replied McCord, "but neither of them have siblings."

"Okay," Buchanan nodded, "but didn't your research into Rollins indicate that he was the school and neighborhood bully?"

"Yeah; but a fifteen year-old picking on a six or seven year-old, for example?"

"It wouldn't be the first time, unfortunately."

"Even so, this updated report," McCord held up a paper, "tends to render your coincidental revelation rather moot."

"Rollins' accident report?"

"Correct," said McCord, "With emphasis on *accident*."

"What's it say?"

McCord held up the report and read aloud, "Although it is unclear exactly how Mister Rollins fell... from the railing itself for some unknown reason, or he climbed over the railing and slipped on the loose rocks beneath his feet... a tragic accident is the likely conclusion."

"Hmm... does that square with your *'how did he get from here to there'* concern?"

"Not exactly," replied McCord, "but then I'm not a forensics expert; just a curious cop."

"Well, crap," Buchanan sighed, "That little *growing up in the same neighborhood* was the only item of note I've come up with on Swenson thus far."

"Are you talking about trying to tie him to Rollins? Or is something else on our mind?"

"That was part of it, but it was more what we discussed a few days ago... looking to identify some of Swenson's external stressors in order to assess his risk of getting pushed over the edge."

"Understood," McCord nodded. He then queried, "Along those lines, I thought you were looking into the various negative comments directed at him about the event on the bridge?"

"I did; and there are plenty of jerk-wads out there slamming Swenson and questioning his manhood," Buchanan replied, "but like I stated earlier I'm not finding any responses that I can attribute to Swenson."

"Maybe Swenson's responding under a nom de plume? Almost no one uses their actual name on some of the sites, like Twitter for example."

"Sure, but how am I supposed to figure out an alias that might be Swenson?"

"Do you want to be a Beat Cop for the rest of your life, or do you want to be an investigator... a detective."

"The latter of course."

"Then get to investigating," McCord pointed.

"You're a hard-ass; you know that?" Buchanan replied as he commenced an internet search.

McCord grinned.

McCord's cell phone rang. He looked at the Caller I.D. – it was a familiar number. "Officer McCord," he spoke as he answered.

"Officer McCord, it's Heather Kincaid," emanated through the phone.

"Yes Ms. Kincaid," McCord glanced over at Buchanan, "What can I do for you?"

"Sorry to bother you, but I found one of those note-poem things from Eric in my purse."

"In your purse?" McCord replied.

"Yes."

"And I'm assuming you don't know how or when he managed to place it there?"

"That's correct," Heather replied, "Which is the reason it has me worried."

"Was the message threatening at all?"

"No... thankfully," Heather replied, "More kind of mystical than anything I suppose." She took a moment, "You know... how he tends to write."

"I understand," replied McCord. "I'd like to take a look at that note. If you're going to be home later how about Officer Buchanan and I stop by?"

"I would appreciate that... thank you."

McCord hung up his phone and exhaled.

"Heather found another note from Swenson?" Buchanan relayed to McCord.

"Yep," McCord replied in a breathy voice.

Buchanan looked at his watch, "Did you want to head over to her place now?"

"Let's give it a half-hour or so."

"In that case I guess I need to get back to these social media..." Buchanan stopped himself as he stared at his computer screen. "Hey, here's something," he said.

"A name that could be Swenson's alias?" McCord replied.

"No; it's a name that jumped out at me for another reason."

"What've you got?" asked McCord as he leaned over to take a look.

"Posts from a *Rollin' Thunder*," Buchanan pointed.

"Rollin' Thunder, eh?" McCord nodded. "You think that could be Rollins?"

"It's worth a shot."

"You check out his posts," stated McCord, "and I'll look into his Twitter and other social media accounts."

"Whoa," commented Buchanan as he scrolled through comments regarding posts about the bridge event.

McCord looked Buchanan's way.

Buchanan looked up from his screen, "This *Rollin' Thunder dude* not only bashes Swenson, but he calls him a *crybaby* and says that he *should have jumped*."

"Holy crap," responded McCord, "Just like the voicemail message Swenson received."

"Yep," Buchanan looked toward McCord, "Do you think he's the mysterious caller?"

"Might take a bit of research to figure that out; he could have used a burner phone," McCord replied. He suddenly stopped his website search, "Hey, according to Rollins' facebook page he identifies his Twitter handle as @Rollin'Thunder."

"Son of a..." Buchanan started, "The coincidences are adding up."

"That's a fact; but with the M.E. ruling Rollins' death an accident..." McCord's voice trailed off as he pondered the potential conundrum.

"But the M.E. can always update his initial ruling based on new evidence, correct?"

"That's true," McCord replied, "But *proving* as much is an entirely different story."

"Yeah," Buchanan sighed. He gazed back at his screen and stated, "Hey, here's an interesting exchange."

"Concerning Rollins' post?"

"Yep. After his 'crybaby' and 'should have jumped' remarks someone responded *'Building oneself up by tearing others down? Sounds like the mantra of a sniveling clown'.*"

The post caught McCord's attention, "A rhyme? Like Swenson's handiwork?" he said.

"That's what jumped out at me," said Buchanan. "But the author's name is 'Pearl of Wisdom'," he said, "And the exchange between these two continues."

"Like they're going after each other?"

"Yep," said Buchanan, who then continued, "Rollin' Thunder replies *'Sticking up for the crybaby are you? Someone should kick your sorry ass as well'* and then Pearl of Wisdom responds back *'You talk the big talk, but do you walk the walk?'.*"

"Hmm... that last response rhymes, but it's a fairly common comeback," noted McCord. "Maybe it's not Swenson's handiwork after all."

"Well, here's the last part, let me know what you think," Buchanan replied, "Rollin' Thunder says *'Name the time and the place and I'll be there; we'll see who's all-talk-and-no-action'*, and then here's Pearl of Wisdom's somewhat cryptic response, *'Be on the Lookout, The time is High Noon; Not Gary Cooper, Just the neighborhood goon'.*"

The words hit McCord like a smack upside the head, "You've got to be kidding me?!" he responded as he scrambled over to Buchanan's monitor to see the words for himself.

Buchanan had not expected such a reaction from McCord. "Right here," he pointed when McCord leaned in.

"Maybe I'm reading more into it than is truly there," McCord said, "but there is no reason to capitalize the word 'lookout' in that context."

"Unless they are referring to Lookout Point?" Buchanan wondered.

"Exactly."

"But what about the fact that 'high noon' is capitalized as well?"

"Since it's the name of a movie *starring* Gary Cooper, it makes sense to capitalize those words," replied McCord.

"So, it's a movie reference?" Buchanan queried.

"Perhaps; but noon would also fit within the timeline that Rollins fell to his death."

"And the fact that 'neighborhood goon' is NOT capitalized?"

"I think that is purposeful as well... to *minimalize* the intended target."

"You know, you're sounding like a profiler," said Buchanan.

McCord laughed, "I thought for sure you were going to say 'conspiracy theorist'."

Buchanan grinned, "Along those lines... any *'theories'*," he said with air-quotes, "regarding the author's name 'Pearl of Wisdom'?"

"As a matter of fact," McCord replied as he grabbed a sheet of paper off of his desk. "It didn't dawn on me until you read the posts, but Swenson's grandmother's first name," he pointed at the sheet, "Pearl."

"You're thinking his grandmother is this person 'Pearl of Wisdom'?"

"Heck no," replied McCord, "I think Swenson chose the nom de plume, and he's savvy enough to keep us from tracing it to him."

"We may not have the resources," replied Buchanan, "but couldn't we kick it over to the State Crime Lab's Cyber Unit?"

"With Rollins' death being ruled an accident there's no way the Captain would approve us taking this to the Cyber Unit."

"Yeah, I guess you're right," Buchanan sighed. He suddenly perked up, "What if we can get Swenson to admit that he's this 'Pearl of Wisdom' person?"

"Even so, all we'd have is verbal sparring between a couple of knuckleheads," McCord replied, "There's no proof right now that Swenson had anything to do with Rollins' death."

"Damn…" Buchanan replied.

"Yep," McCord replied. He looked at his watch, "What say we go see what Ms. Heather Kincaid has for us?"

26

Rap-rap-rap Heather almost jumped out of her flip-flops; stoked by the fact that she was literally standing right next to the door and had not heard a single step approaching. Still holding the watering can she'd been using on her entryway plants, she realized her hands were shaking.

She nuzzled up to the door to peer through the peephole – it was blocked. Her heart raced. She put down the watering can and grabbed her cell phone. She dialed "9", then "1", and stood ready to dial one more "1".

"Who is it?" Heather called out to whoever was on the other side of the door.

"Ms. Kincaid, it's Officers McCord and Buchanan," the muffled voice of McCord replied.

Recognizing the voice, Heather slowly opened the door. "Why did you block the peephole?" she asked.

"We didn't," McCord replied as he pointed toward the door.

Heather looked over and spied a scrap of paper taped over the peephole. She swung the door fully open. The scrap was blank on the side facing out. She grasped and peeled it off the door. She turned it around to discover writing. It read…

"What if I fall in love?
It has been so long.
Like a curse from above,
What went wrong?"

Heather dropped her hand and paused in thought.

"Another poem from Mister Swenson?" McCord inquired.

"Yes," Heather replied as she handed the scrap to McCord.

McCord read the scrap, "Does this mean anything to you?" he said to Heather as he handed the scrap to Buchanan.

"Lyrics from another song," Heather replied, "but the last two lines have been changed."

"What's different?"

"The original lyrics were *'like a GIFT from above, IT CAN'T BE wrong'.*"

Buchanan, holding the scrap, looked over to Heather, "So, it has been changed from 'gift' to 'curse'," he said, "and instead of him saying that 'it can't be wrong' he now asks 'what went wrong'?"

"That's correct," Heather replied. Her lower lip and chin began to quiver, "So, besides asking what went wrong he is also saying that our relationship wasn't something special, but instead was a curse."

Both McCord and Buchanan were at a loss for words. They decided to remain silent and give Heather a moment.

Heather took a breath. "Anyway," she continued, "As you might have gathered, this is *not* the note that I had called you about... the one I found in my purse."

"Speaking of..." McCord prompted.

"Oh, of course," said Heather, "Let me get that for you." She spun around and vanished. As she returned she was unfolding a sheet of paper. "I'm not sure why Eric buried this in my purse," she stated as she handed the paper to McCord, "It's not about me... or about us... it's like he's talking to himself."

McCord scanned the paper; it read...

Will I enter those hallowed halls

when the final curtain falls?

*

Will purgatory be my destination
when the funeral train departs the station?

*

Or will the gates of Hell be beckoning
upon my day of reckoning?"

"Hmm..." McCord murmured as he contemplated the note. He handed it to Buchanan.

"See what I mean?" Heather directed to McCord.

McCord nodded... and pondered.

Buchanan handed the paper back to McCord. "Interesting," he commented, "Any ideas?"

"Well, here's a thought..." McCord replied. "The way I read it, the first part asks if he will be going to Heaven upon his death, implying he feels that he is essentially a good soul.

"The second part asks if he is destined for Purgatory, which, to my understanding anyway, some theologians believe is where you end up when you commit suicide.

"And the third part asks if he will be going straight to Hell, which one can only assume means that he may be planning, or end up committing, an evil act."

"That's an intriguing notion," Buchanan nodded.

Heather grew pale as she considered the possible intent of Swenson's writing, "You think Eric might be planning an evil act?" she directed to McCord.

"Hard to say at this point, I'm merely speculating as to what he might be trying to say," McCord replied, "I think our best bet," he nodded toward Buchanan, "is to talk to Mister Swenson and inquire as to the intent behind his words."

Heather stood in stunned silence, staring off in the distance as she contemplated thoughts she had never considered.

"When exactly did he leave this in your purse?" McCord asked Heather.

"I'm not really sure. I found it a couple of days ago, but it was buried in the bottom of my purse," Heather replied, "As if he didn't want me to find it right away."

"Hmm…" McCord nodded, "Can you come up with a timeframe?"

Heather pondered for a moment, "Let me think… I walked and jogged the bridge on Friday and again on Sunday," she replayed the events in her mind, "So it had to be either one of those times when I left my purse at home, or he snuck in while I was either asleep or in the shower."

"And you're sure about the timeframe?"

"Yes," Heather replied, "Because I switched purses Friday morning before I left on my jog."

"Okay, that helps… thanks," said McCord. "Oh, and of course we will need to retain these," he said as he held up the notes.

"I understand," Heather replied.

27

"This thing with Swenson and poems, or rhymes, or whatever is kind of strange, don't you think?" said Buchanan as McCord and he were driving toward Eric Swenson's apartment.

"I agree; but his apparent need to make some kind of poetic statement could be leaving unintended clues," replied McCord, "especially if he turns out to be this 'Pearl of Wisdom' character."

"You've got a point there," Buchanan nodded.

- ❊ -

Rap-rap-rap Buchanan knocked on the door of Eric Swenson's apartment – McCord standing nearby.

The Officers heard faint footsteps approaching from the other side of the door, followed by brief silence, and then a muffled, "You've got to be kidding me!"

McCord and Buchanan looked at each other. "Apparently he's not too happy to see us," Buchanan commented.

The door slowly opened. "Officers," said Swenson.

The Officers scanned Swenson over. "More rugby?" inquired McCord.

"What can I say," Swenson replied, "I enjoy a good scrum."

"Yeah... about that," McCord responded, "There's something of a contradiction with your earlier statement."

"My earlier statement?" said Swenson.

"The other day you said you were all beat to hell because of rugby," stated McCord, "but it was obvious you had just thrown on your dirty and grungy, yet perfectly dry, outfit."

"And we checked Gig Harbor RFC's schedule," added Buchanan, "Your rugby match was the day before."

"Wow, you guys really are top notch investigators," Swenson sarcastically replied, "but you completely misunderstood my statement."

"In that case, how about you educate us?" said McCord.

"I didn't say I had *just been* in a rugby match," Swenson replied, "I said that rugby was the reason I was all beat up."

"So, you just happen to prance around in your rugby outfit on days that you don't have a match?" said Buchanan.

"I wasn't *'prancing around'*," Swenson tersely replied, "I was just getting ready to jump in the shower when you guys knocked; so after I saw that it was you two at the door I went back to the bedroom and grabbed something to throw on, which happened to be my rugby outfit that was draped over a chair."

After processing Swenson's response the Officers realized they may have jumped to conclusions regarding Swenson's previous actions, but they maintained their poker faces... along with their skepticism.

"But if you prefer," Swenson added, "in the future I can just answer the door in *all my glory*," he gestured toward his crotch.

"That won't be necessary," stated McCord.

"I guess that means we're done here, right?" Swenson replied.

"Not even close," McCord responded.

Swenson crossed his arms, "It's your dime," he said.

"The other day you said you didn't know Caleb Rollins, the gentleman who fell to his death right around the time that you were on the bridge."

"Yeah... so?"

"Turns out that you grew up in that same neighborhood, and apparently he was known as the local bully."

"I remember a much older kid who was always acting tough," Swenson replied, "Are you telling me this Rollins dude is that guy?"

"So it appears."

Swenson snickered, "You guys must love grasping at straws; especially since I read that the dude's death was ruled to be an accident."

Buchanan jumped into the conversations, "Rollins, and hence *you*, came to our attention because of some interesting posts regarding your event on the bridge a week ago."

Swenson shook his head, "Okay, now you've totally lost me."

"You ever hear the name *Rollin' Thunder?*" asked McCord.

"What is that; the name of a Monster Truck or something?" Swenson replied.

"It's Caleb Rollins' social media alias," McCord replied, "and he posted some rather inflammatory comments regarding your dilemma."

"If you say so," Swenson shrugged.

"What initially caught our attention was a comment he made that mirrored a statement you gave us."

"And that was...?"

"He called you a crybaby," replied McCord, "and said that you should've jumped."

"Hmm, just like the asshole who left the voicemail."

"Exactly."

"Go figure that *he* would be the one to fall to his death," stated Swenson, "Talk about Karma..."

"Interestingly enough," said McCord, "that's not all."

"You traced the call to him?"

"No; this had to do with some intriguing responses to his comments," said McCord, "And those responses happened to bear your 'signature'."

"My signature?" stated Swenson, "I thought a *'signature'*," he said with air-quotes, "had to do with the M.O. of a crime scene; you know... 'displays the victims in a certain way', 'hog ties them', 'leaves a symbol at the scene like the Zodiac killer'... those sorts of things?"

"How ironic that you should mention the Zodiac killer," replied McCord, "Another part of the Zodiac's *'signature'* were the coded messages he would relay to newspapers, like the infamous Zee-three-forty cypher."

"And how is that *'ironic'* in relation to me?"

"Certain responses to Rollin' Thunder's messages were in rhyme; just like your notes and text to Heather," McCord replied, "And they also appeared to portend Rollins' demise."

"My so-called 'notes' to Heather were lyrics, so of course they rhymed," Swenson replied, "I told you that a week ago."

"You mean like the scrap you placed over the peephole of her door?"

"Sure, I left that," Swenson admitted, "but hey, it's not like I violated a restraining order."

"According to Heather you changed some of the words."

"I was merely trying to make a point."

"And how about the paper you left in Heather's purse?" asked Buchanan.

"It was just a bit of self-reflection that I wanted to share," Swenson replied.

"Then why not share it in person instead of sneaking in and burying it in the bottom of her purse?"

"I didn't *'sneak in'*; I have a key," Swenson said. "She wasn't home when I stopped by, so I placed it somewhere I was sure she'd get it."

"Since your engagement is on-hold don't you think you should return her key?" stated McCord.

"Hey, if she wants me to return the key, all she has to do is say so."

"The *self-reflection* you mentioned in that note seems to show that you are struggling with your potential future… your potential demise," stated McCord.

"What, you're a psychologist now?" Swenson responded.

"No… just observant."

"Oh really?" said Swenson, "And what's your observation?"

"You seemed to be wondering whether you would ultimately end up in Heaven, or in Purgatory, or perhaps in Hell."

"Don't we all?"

"I don't think most of us consider our final destination to be Hell unless we have performed, or intend to perform, some evil act."

"Yeah, well… when you have a life that seems to be nothing more than a recurring pile of dog shit," Swenson replied, "that particular option becomes the most likely scenario." He pondered for a moment and added, "Besides; as always, you guys are taking my poetic words literally."

"That's what you said on the bridge," Buchanan responded, "and as soon as we walked away you turned around and climbed the tower."

Swenson glared at Buchanan. "That was your fault for daring me!" he pointed.

Buchanan was tempted to chide Swenson for his *'he made me do it'* defense, but thought better of it.

"Be that as it may," McCord jumped in, "As I said earlier, the responses to Rollin' Thunder's posts were akin to portending his future."

"And how is that?" said Swenson.

"They said to *be on the lookout*… as in 'Lookout Point'," replied McCord, "at high noon… which was around the time he fell to his death. And referred to him as the neighborhood goon… as in 'the neighborhood bully'."

"You guys are hilarious," Swenson replied, "It sounds like you're trying to connect non-existent dots to fit some nefarious theory behind, what was ruled to be, *an accident.*"

"I take it you're not admitting to being the author?"

"Was my name attached to it?"

"The author's alias is 'Pearl of Wisdom'," replied McCord, "And it just so happens that your grandmother's name is Pearl."

"You think my *grandmother* is the source?" Swenson laughed, "She's in her seventies and can barely figure out how to send emails using a tablet my aunt gave her."

"Actually, we're thinking that *you* are the author and you decided to honor your grandmother by selecting her name as part of your alias."

"Sorry to disappoint," Swenson replied, "I guess you'll have to find some other poor sap to embroil in your conspiracy theory."

"Alright then," McCord responded, "Thanks for your time."

Swenson stood there momentarily, shook his head, and then shut the door. The Officers turned and walked away.

28

July 25th

"Have you ever had another jurisdiction want to talk to you about one of their open cases?" Buchanan asked McCord as they were driving along Highway 16 northwest toward Port Orchard.

"Only those that were a separate jurisdiction, yet were still local," McCord replied.

"How do you mean?"

"The State Patrol for cases along the highway that runs through Gig Harbor; and the bridge of course," McCord clarified, "Plus, the Pierce County Sheriff's Department."

"Oh yeah... duh," replied Buchanan. "But no other counties like Kitsap or Mason?"

"Correct."

"Since the Captain didn't have any details to share, I don't suppose you have any idea as to why Kitsap County law enforcement wants to talk to us?"

"The only thing that makes sense to me," McCord replied, "is perhaps their recent murder has provided some potential leads pointing toward our neck of the woods?"

"Yeah, I guess so," Buchanan replied. "I have to admit, I'm definitely curious."

"You and me both," said McCord, "Who knows... perhaps we'll get read-in on something that would normally be outside of *our need-to-know.*"

"That would be cool."

"Then again; it could be nothing more than a *'be on the lookout for'*..."

The Officers wheeled their cruiser into the parking area of the Kitsap County Municipality... the Courthouse, Sheriff's Office, County Jail, County Commissioners, Assessor's Office, Auditor's Office, Records Office, and more.

Walking into the Sheriff's Office McCord and Buchanan immediately made eye contact with a professionally-attired woman.

"Good morning," stated McCord as he approached the woman, "We're..."

"Officers McCord and Buchanan from the Gig Harbor Police Department?" the woman interrupted.

"As a matter of fact..."

"Detective Nash," the woman once again interrupted and held out her hand.

"Nice to meet you," said McCord as he shook hands with the Detective.

"Likewise," Detective Nash responded. She then exchanged pleasantries with Officer Buchanan as well.

"Detective," stated Buchanan as he shook hands.

"You're probably wondering what this is all about," stated the Detective, "Let's go to the Conference Room and I'll fill you in," she nodded.

"I normally work out of our satellite location in Silverdale," the Detective continued as she walked – the Officers right on her heels, "but I figured our main office here would be more convenient for you gentlemen."

"No problem either way for us," McCord replied.

The trio entered the Conference Room. "Please... have a seat," said the Detective as she sat down; a file folder in front of her.

Now seated, the Detective began... "I understand that you are briefly aware of the murder that happened in the north end of the county a few days ago?"

"Yes," replied McCord, "and ironically, unbeknownst to me at the time, I was in that general area later that evening... attending the service for Justin Coleman in Port Gamble."

"I had planned to be in attendance as well," stated the Detective, "but ended up drawing the short straw when it came to deciding who could attend, and who had to stay and hold down the fort."

"I understand."

"Anyway," the Detective continued, "We had another one yesterday; this one was out in Seabeck."

"Another murder?"

"That's correct."

"Same M.O.?" asked Buchanan.

"No," replied the Detective, "Thus, as near as we can tell, the two murders are unrelated."

"You're sure it's a murder and not an accident?" said McCord.

"Not officially; but the Deputy Coroner is pretty confident in her initial assessment, so we're treating it as such unless, and until, autopsy results indicate otherwise."

"Reminds me of our case with Caleb Rollins," stated McCord.

"But in the reverse, correct?" remarked the Detective, "Initial indications leaned toward an accident, and the ultimate conclusion corroborated that assessment?"

"That's true," replied Buchanan, "but there are a few things that keep us wondering, even though we have no proof of foul play."

"Interesting..." stated the Detective. "That kind of plays into one of my reasons for asking you two here," she added.

"How's that?" replied McCord.

"You're still recognizing inconsistencies and-or potential evidence even after most would sign things off as *case closed*'... for one," the Detective replied. "And for two: How you took a few pieces of information about a missing person and managed to recognize them as *clues* leading to a would-be bridge jumper... not everyone would have made that tie. And even those who would've made the tie may not have done so in time to save him."

"We appreciate that," McCord replied.

"So how can we help?" Buchanan added.

"Understand that none of this can interfere with your normal duties," the Detective replied, "but if we have potential leads leaning in your direction I may ask for assistance… within reason of course."

"Of course," McCord replied.

"Or if you simply have some ideas that you want to share," the Detective added, "I would appreciate you sending them my way."

"Absolutely."

"Great; then let me fill you in on our current situation," stated the Detective. She reached into the file folder and extracted a series of photographs. She placed the first one in front of the Officers, "This is the victim at the scene," she stated, "The trauma to the skull being clearly evident."

The Officers nodded concurrence with the Detective's comment.

"This is a close-up of the mandible," the Detective stated as she placed a second photograph in front of the Officers. "It was several yards away," she added.

"As if the killer tossed it?" asked McCord.

"Yes," the Detective replied. "Here's a wider view - the arrows are pointing to the victim, and to the weapon," she stated as she produced another photo.

"Any evidence potentially left on the weapon by the killer?"

"Yes and no," the Detective replied. "No DNA; but there were small pieces of leather," she added, "indicating that the perp wore gloves."

"Have you determined the reason the victim was in the area?" asked Buchanan.

"Funny you should ask," stated the Detective as she extracted another photo from the folder. "He lives just up the street… on Iverson," she said, "This is a satellite photo. Here's his house," she pointed, "and the location his body was found."

"Hmm…" McCord started, "The first inclination would be taking a look at his neighbors."

"We haven't officially ruled any of them out, but we've found no direct evidence that would implicate them at this point," said the Detective, "Even though he wasn't the most popular guy in the neighborhood."

"What was their beef with him?"

"Primarily, how he kept his property… or the lack thereof," she stated as she showed another photo. "As you can see it looks like a rundown shack in the midst of a wrecking yard."

"Wow," said Buchanan, "I can see why the neighbors might be displeased."

"And to make matters worse… for us investigators anyway… is that he had a yard sale over the weekend," said the Detective, "Which means an entire platoon of garage sale soldiers, who would not normally be in the area, trampling all over the yard and manhandling would-be evidence."

"So the killer could've left his DNA, and yet would have a perfectly sound reason for it being there," noted McCord.

"Precisely."

"Talk about a roadblock," stated Buchanan.

"You've got that right," replied the Detective.

"Any chance it was a robbery gone bad?" asked McCord.

"His wallet, full of cash and credit cards, was still on him."

"So he was specifically targeted."

"Or he really pissed someone off."

"Anything missing from his home?" asked Buchanan.

"Almost impossible to tell," replied the Detective, "With a yard sale going on you don't know if the usual items… televisions, stereos, jewelry, power tools, etcetera… were stolen, or merely had been sold as part of the sale." The Detective paused for a moment and added, "But the strong box he used as his cash register was still on a shelf in the garage… full of bills."

"Do you think the perp might have been one of his yard sale customers?" said McCord, "His *last* customer?"

"We're looking at that possibility."

"The yard sale also could have provided the perp an opportunity to stake out the guy and property without drawing suspicion," McCord pondered.

"You're absolutely right," said the Detective, "That option is also on our radar screen. But here's another wrinkle: It's not as if the potential customers were those folks who happened to drive by Stottlemeyer or Iverson Roads and saw his hand-painted sign," she said as she pulled out a picture of a chunk of plywood that said 'yard sale' in red spray paint, "he also advertised it on social media."

"So potential suspects, or witnesses, could have shown up from anywhere."

"Yep."

"Whew," Buchanan shook his head, "Anything else?"

"Forensics has verified that the animal mandible found at the scene was, in fact, the murder weapon," replied the Detective. "With that in mind, considering the various horses, cows, and llamas in the area we were sure that it had to be a weapon of opportunity…"

McCord inadvertently interrupted, "Are you implying that it did not originate from one of the nearby ranches?"

"That's correct. It turns out that the mandible is from either a donkey or a mule. None of the ranchers have such an animal within their stables."

"The killer brought a mandible with him to use as a weapon?"

"Apparently so; as crazy as that sounds," replied the Detective. "Needless to say we're getting the word out to all of the counties here on the Olympic Peninsula for such ranches. It's a longshot I realize, but you can't find what you don't seek."

"And you'd like us to see if such ranches exist in our area?" said McCord.

"Yes; along with any future leads that might fall within your jurisdiction," replied the Detective, "And, as I mentioned earlier, I welcome any thoughts and ideas you might have."

McCord pondered for a moment. "Do you have any more on the murder in Seabeck?" he asked.

"Not at this time," said the Detective, "Other than the fact that the victim was face-down in mudflats. He has a head wound, but we think that's from falling on the stones on the beach since he appears to have died from asphyxiation." She glanced back and forth between the Officers, "I'll provide updates as applicable."

The Officers nodded comprehension.

The Detective stood and extended her hand. "And that's all I had for now; thank you very much for coming out here."

The Officers stood and shook hands with the Detective. "It was our pleasure," stated McCord. Buchanan smiled agreement.

- ❊ -

"Pretty cool for a couple of Beat Cops to get asked to help out on a case in another jurisdiction," Buchanan commented as McCord and he were driving back toward Gig Harbor.

"I don't know about you, but it makes me want to strive for a future as a detective," stated McCord.

"I'll second that motion."

McCord sat in quiet contemplation when his demeanor suddenly changed, "Crap!" he blurted out and grabbed his cell phone.

"What is it?" Buchanan stated as he briefly glanced over at McCord while still keeping an eye on the highway and his hands on the wheel.

McCord held up his finger in a 'just a sec' gesture while his phone was nestled against his ear. "Detective Nash," he spoke into the phone, "This is Officer McCord."

"Yes, Officer," the Detective replied.

"You may be already looking into this, but something just dawned on me, and since you hadn't mentioned it I thought I'd throw it out there."

"Sure, what have you got?"

"Last Labor Day weekend my wife and I were attending the Blackberry Festival on the Bremerton waterfront and one of the activities they had for kids was a donkey ride," McCord stated, "You know… several donkeys going around in circles in a small corral… kind of a *Live Merry Go-Round* if you will."

"And you're thinking that if we get hold of festival organizers we can find out where the proprietor is located?"

"That was my thought, yes," McCord replied. "And even if they aren't the source of the mandible found at the scene, they might be able to provide you other prospective ranches."

"That's a great idea," replied the Detective. "In fact, that just gave me another idea: area ranchers who exhibit their livestock at the County Fair," she added. "Bringing you two in on this is already paying dividends… thank you."

"You're welcome," McCord responded and then hung up his phone.

Buchanan glanced over to McCord, "I take it that Detective Nash had not thought of that?"

"Apparently not," McCord replied.

"I don't know how you come up with this stuff."

"To be honest, sometimes I even surprise my own self."

29

"Well, well, well… it's the cross-jurisdictional duo," extolled Captain Denise Prescott as Officers McCord and Buchanan strolled into the Gig Harbor Police Station.

"Hey Cap," McCord grinned.

"I talked to Detective Nash and she said you all had a very productive meeting," said the Captain, "and that you had already provided her with some potentially relevant information."

"We're looking forward to assisting in any way that we can," McCord replied.

"Obviously you'll have to work that around your normal duties," stated the Captain, "But be sure to keep me in the loop."

"Yes ma'am."

The Captain departed the area and the Officers sat down at their respective desks. McCord pulled out his memo pad to review their conversation with Detective Nash; Buchanan logged on to his computer.

"While the Detective is trying to run down the owners of that donkey ride from the Blackberry Festival," Buchanan commented as he typed, "I'm thinking we could do a little research here in our locality."

"Good point," McCord replied. He thought for a moment and added, "Speaking of research; did you ever come up with anything on that Smart Car or whatever that Heather had mentioned the day Rollins fell to his death?"

"You just can't let the Rollins case go, can you?"

"What can I say," replied McCord, "I'm like a dog with a bone… gnawing at that last sliver of meat before I bury it."

"I did a search for all similar micro-sized vehicles since a number of manufacturers build those little buggers," replied Buchanan, "The Scion iQ, for example, was a literal clone of the Smart Car."

"Wait a minute," McCord looked befuddled, "You're telling me that Scion came up with a car named '*I-Q*'," he said with air-quotes, "to compete with the '*Smart*' car?"

"Marketing *genius*, right?" Buchanan laughed.

"Ugh," McCord rolled his eyes.

"Anyway," said Buchanan, "It was a dead end."

"That figures," McCord responded. "Hey, since you're logged on, how about taking a look at Jared Paget's post on social media about his yard sale?"

"Sure," Buchanan replied as he manipulated his keyboard and mouse. "This guy is definitely NOT a marketing genius," he said as he reviewed the post, "His '*catchy photo to draw the reader in*' is a picture of his spray-painted 'yard sale' sign with a bunch of crap just lying around the yard in the background."

"Implying that his *big sale* is essentially an attempt to get rid of his stockpile of junk?"

"Yep. In fact, as I scroll through the various comments that exact term is used, along with other similar descriptors."

McCord rolled his chair over to Buchanan's desk. Buchanan pointed at his computer screen, "Check it out," he said, "'*Mostly just a bunch of junk*', '*don't waste your time*', '*I've seen better stuff at an illegal dump site*'."

"Hard to believe someone would've been so pissed about nothing but junk that they'd kill the guy," said McCord.

"Maybe there was something there that they wanted, but it wasn't for sale... something that Paget *refused* to sell?"

"That would make a lot more sense."

"But that still begs the question..." Buchanan noted, "Why the hell did they have an animal mandible with them?"

"That aspect of the mystery might remain unsolved until a suspect is in custody."

"So basically our social media search here resulted in a whole lot of nothing."

"For us perhaps," replied McCord, "But Detective Nash and her team might be digging up some important nuggets that we're not privy to."

McCord's desk phone rang – he could see by the Caller I.D. that it was the Reception Desk on the com-line. He picked up the handset from its cradle; "Officer McCord," he said into the phone.

"Officer McCord, a gentleman with his teenage son is here," echoed through the phone, "He said that he might have some information regarding the Caleb Rollins accident."

"Really?" McCord perked up, "Go ahead and send them through, would you?"

As McCord hung up his phone, a buzz followed by a *click* rang out at the inner door. In walked a father and his son, whom appeared to be about fourteen years old. The boy looked timid; as if he got caught leaving a flaming sack of dog poop on a neighbor's stoop and dad was going to 'scare him straight' by taking him to confess, in person, to the cops.

McCord and Buchanan both stood to greet the duo. The gentleman extended his hand as he approached the Officers; the boy dropped his head down. "Officers McCord and Buchanan?" the gentleman asked; "Bruce Carlton." He then nodded toward his son, "This is my son, Devon." Devon looked up briefly; and then back toward the floor.

"Officer McCord," replied McCord as he shook Carlton's hand; and then extended his hand toward Devon. Carlton nudged Devon. Devon looked back up and limply shook McCord's hand. Buchanan mimicked McCord's actions.

"What can we do for you?" McCord asked of Carlton.

"News reports over the weekend asked for anyone who might have been in the area of the Narrows Bridge or Lookout Point last Friday in the early afternoon who might have seen anything, to contact the authorities," Carlton replied.

"And you saw something?" McCord asked, "But didn't think to let us know until now?"

"Not me..." Carlton nodded toward Devon, "My son." "And we didn't come forward sooner because he didn't realize that he might have seen something," he added.

"You two were at Lookout Point around that time, your son saw something, but you didn't?"

"I wasn't there," Carlton responded, "just him," he nodded.

"I'm a bit confused, Sir," McCord replied, "You're going to have to fill in the blanks."

"My son and I were out at The Narrows Golf Club that day... Friday, and he got bored around the seventh green," Carlton replied, "I told him that he could take the golf cart for a spin around the course and to meet us... my caddy and me... at the ninth hole and then we'd grab some lunch before continuing on to the back nine."

"Are you implying that he drove the cart to Lookout Point?"

"I didn't know it at the time, but yes... he took a joy ride along the paved walking-trail that runs between the golf course and Lookout Point," Carlton replied. "He got caught spilling the beans to one of his friends last night, and I told him we needed to come by and talk to you folks today."

McCord turned to Devon, "What all did you see, Devon?"

"It didn't seem like anything, but my dad said I should tell you anyway," Devon replied.

"And what was that?"

"I drove into the parking lot... you know... there at Lookout Point," Devon said, "And over at the far end of the lot, near the railing, were a couple of guys... it seemed like they were arguing. Anyway, I did a quick turn-around in the cart... I mean heck, there's nothing interesting in a parking lot... and when I looked back to where the two guys were; only *one* guy was there."

"You're saying that when you drove into the lot there were *two* guys, and after you turned around about what… maybe a minute later, there was only *one* guy?"

"Yep…" Devon replied. "And *less than* a minute," he added.

"But you didn't see what happened to the guy, or between the two men?"

"Nope… just one minute he was there, and the next minute he was gone."

"Do you think you could describe either of the men?"

"Oh, heck no… they were too far away."

"Could you hear what they were arguing about?"

"Do you know how loud a golf cart is?" Devon responded, "I could barely hear myself think."

"Then what makes you think the men were arguing?"

"The way they were pointing at each other and flapping their arms around," Devon replied. "I've seen plenty of that in the schoolyard over the years… I know what arguing looks like."

"I guess you probably would," McCord nodded. Something suddenly dawned on him, "Did you happen to see a bicycle nearby?"

"Hmm… now that I think of it, there might have been one there."

McCord's eyes grew wide open, "Any chance you could describe it?"

Devon shook his head, "Nope."

"When you looked back and saw only the one guy; was the bicycle still there?"

Devon stared off in the distance, recalling the event, "Yeah… I think so."

McCord and Buchanan looked at each other with raised eyebrows.

McCord returned his gaze toward Devon, "Does that mean you didn't see him ride away?"

"I didn't look back after that."

"I understand," McCord replied. He looked over to Buchanan and then back to Carlton and Devon, "Anything else?" he said to the duo.

Both Mister Carlton and Devon shook their heads NO.

"Alright then," McCord said as he handed his card to Carlton, "Thank you very much for the information. If you think of anything else, please don't hesitate to call."

"Our pleasure," said Carlton as he reached out to shake hands with McCord and then Buchanan. He and Devon then turned around and exited the area.

Buchanan turned to McCord, "Holy crap!" he said, "What do you make of there being a bicycle at the scene?"

"Another piece of a crazy-ass jigsaw," McCord replied.

"And how much you wanna bet that Devon's golf cart is the 'Smart Car'," he said with air-quotes, "that Heather saw?"

"I'm not taking that bet," McCord replied.

"So, now what?"

"It's probably not enough to get Rollins' death ruled to be something other than accidental, but we should pass it on to the Captain," McCord replied.

"Shit just keeps getting more and more curious; if not downright strange," noted Buchanan.

"That's a fact."

"Are you thinking about taking another run at Swenson?"

"It's tempting," McCord replied, "but before we lose any more momentum on the Jared Paget case let's get back to digging into it."

"I'm one step ahead of you," said Buchanan as he performed a few mouse clicks on his computer.

"What're you looking for?"

"I've transitioned from the man himself and his yard sale; to horse, donkey, mule ranches and the like."

"What about farmers and ranchers who exhibit their livestock at the County Fair?"

"Since that would be under the Detective's jurisdiction," replied Buchanan, "I'm thinking she's got one of her folks working that angle."

"Good point."

"Hey, here's something," said Buchanan as he looked up from his computer, "A business called *Donkey Rides 4 Kids*. The website says they provide donkey rides at various events such as fairs, festivals, and private parties."

"Where're they located?"

"Just north of Gig Harbor proper," Buchanan replied. "What say we go pay them a visit?"

"Let me run it by the Captain," said McCord, "And if she gives us the thumbs-up… we're outta here."

30

Officers Buchanan and McCord pulled their cruiser into the long driveway of Walker Ranch, the home of Henry and Phyllis Walker, proprietors of *Donkey Rides 4 Kids*. The Officers realized that their quest to discover the source of the murder weapon used in neighboring Kitsap County was likely an exercise in futility, but as Detective Nash had pointed out, you can't find what you don't seek. McCord also figured that each person of interest you remove from the equation narrows the pool of suspects. But with the murder scene being fairly close to the Kingston-Edmonds ferry, along with the Hood Canal Bridge, a more troubling conclusion came to mind: the entirety of the Puget Sound area, including the Kitsap and Olympic Peninsulas, was in-play. His optimism waned as he pondered the notion.

Having parked and exited their cruiser, the Officers stepped onto the porch of the Walker home. McCord took a breath and rapped on the door. A mid-fifties gentleman wearing a cowboy hat opened the door; he was surprised at the sight of two uniformed police officers.

"Mister Henry Walker?" stated McCord.

"Yes," Henry replied, "What can I do for you gentlemen?"

Before McCord could reply, a feminine voice rang out from inside the house, "Who is it, dear?"

Henry turned his head to respond to the voice, "A couple of police officers."

"Police officers?" the woman replied as she scurried toward the door.

The woman sidled up next to Henry. "My wife Phyllis," Henry said to the Officers as he introduced his wife; an early-fifties woman, hair pulled back in a pony-tail, appearing as if she'd just finished up a hard day's work in the corral. She smiled at the Officers.

"Officers McCord and Buchanan with the Gig Harbor Police Department," McCord stated.

"How can we help you gents?" Phyllis asked.

"This may seem like an odd question, so I'll just cut to the chase," McCord replied. "Is it possible that someone purchased a mandible from you folks?" He then added, "Specifically; a donkey mandible from one of your deceased animals?"

The couple looked confused. "That's why you're here?" Henry responded, "About a donkey mandible?"

"I'm afraid so," said McCord.

"Ironically, there was a gentleman from a theatre group," Henry started and then turned to his wife, "What was the name of that group, Hon?"

"Peninsula Theatre Artists," said Phyllis.

"Yeah, that's it," said Henry. "Anyway; he was here several days ago asking about one."

"Did he say why?" asked Buchanan.

"He said he wanted it for an upcoming performance of 'Samson & Delilah'," Phyllis replied. "I can't wait to see it!" she beamed.

McCord and Buchanan perked up. "Do you have the gentleman's name?" asked McCord.

"Let me check our files," Phyllis replied as she dropped out of sight. "She should just be a moment," Henry commented. The Officers nodded.

"Here it is..." stated Phyllis as she returned with a receipt in hand, "Danny Vogel."

"Do you have an address or phone number?" said McCord.

"No; but if you contact the theatre group I'm sure they'd have the info."

"An animal mandible seems like an odd request," Buchanan directed to the couple.

"First time for us," said Phyllis. "But his reason made sense," Henry added.

"And you just happened to have one to give him?" said McCord.

"Well, when you operate a ranch for over twenty years you have the unfortunate occasion of losing an animal from time to time," Phyllis replied. "Mostly due to old age, sometimes due to illness," Henry added. "We've even had trouble with a bear, a cougar, and coyotes over the years," Phyllis finished.

"I'm curious," said Buchanan, "How much does an animal mandible go for?"

"We didn't really have a set price," said Henry, "We just asked for a donation for two kids to ride the donkeys at the upcoming Blackberry Festival."

"He was happy to oblige," said Phyllis, "In fact, he made a 'six kids' donation."

"Forgive me, Officers," Henry started, "But why are you asking about a donkey mandible?"

"Yes," Phyllis added, "Having a gentleman ask for one was strange enough to start with, but having the police asking about it is even more curious."

"Unfortunately," said McCord, "We are not at liberty to share that information at this time."

Henry and Phyllis' mild curiosity took a sudden leap to concern. "I understand… I guess," Henry sighed.

McCord extended his hand to Phyllis and then Henry, "Thank you very much," he said. Buchanan exchanged handshakes with the couple as well.

The Officers jumped in their cruiser and sat momentarily. "I can only imagine what is going through their heads right now," remarked McCord, "Two cops showing up, asking about an animal mandible, and telling them that we can't share the reason we're asking."

"No kidding," replied Buchanan, "I'm guessing they are either somewhat dumbfounded, or completely freaked-out."

McCord reflected about the couple, "Those two have obviously been together a long time."

"Based on them saying they've had the ranch for twenty-odd years?"

"Based on them being on the same wavelength so much that it's as if they're sharing a single brain," McCord grinned.

"You mean how they kept finishing each other's sentence?"

"Even more than that," said McCord, "One starts a sentence, the other adds the middle part, and then the first one finishes it."

"Pretty entertaining, huh?"

"Hilarious," replied McCord as he started to type on the cruiser's laptop.

"You know that you and Kayla do that," grinned Buchanan.

"What? No way," McCord stopped his computer search.

"Yep," Buchanan nodded. "In fact, when you tell her the story I bet she says the same thing."

McCord shook his head as he had returned to manipulating the laptop. "Okay, I found the theatre group's social media page and they list a Danny Vogel as a member," he said. "And a Gig Harbor Resident search shows a Daniel Vogel who lives just a couple of miles from here."

Buchanan started the car. "What say we go see if he's our guy?" he said as he selected DRIVE and hit the gas.

"Absolutely."

– * –

A man noticed a police cruiser pull up to the curb in front of his house. *"I wonder what's going on out there?"* he thought to himself as he approached the front window to get a better look. To his surprise, the policemen were walking toward his front door. He walked over and opened the door before the policemen had a chance to knock.

"Mister Daniel Vogel?" said McCord to the gentleman in the doorway.

"Most people call me Danny," replied the man, "But yes, that would be me; what can I do for you?"

"And you're associated with The Peninsula Theatre Group?" said Buchanan.

"That's correct," Danny replied. He was trying to wrap his head around the reason for the police showing up at his door and asking about the theatre group, but he had no clue as to what that might be.

"I understand you purchased an animal mandible from the Walker Ranch up the road here?" McCord directed to Danny.

"What??" Danny responded, "Why would I do that?"

"The proprietors of the ranch said you wanted it for an upcoming play," said Buchanan.

"What play?"

"Samson & Delilah."

"That's crazy!" said Danny. "For one: I never made such a purchase; and for two: there's no Samson & Delilah performance coming up at any of the local theatres," he added, "I can give you the schedules for all the local playhouses for the next year if you'd like. Heck, I can even get you those in Kitsap."

"Then how do you explain the proprietors having your name as the purchaser?" said McCord.

"Beats the hell out of me," Danny shrugged.

"You're telling us that someone purchased the mandible using your name?"

"Obviously that's the case."

"Any idea why someone would implicate you in this?"

"Implicate me in *what?*" a now-frustrated Danny replied. "And why the heck is there such concern about a stupid animal mandible?"

McCord grabbed his cell phone and brought up a picture of the mandible from the Kitsap County murder scene. He held it in front of Danny, "A mandible was used as a weapon this past Sunday, but did not come from the area where the crime occurred, so we're looking at all possible options," he said, "And just our luck, someone purchased a mandible right up the road here, under your name, the day before the attack."

Danny stood in stunned silence.

"With all that in mind," Buchanan directed at Danny, "Where were you on Sunday?"

"I told you I didn't purchase the stupid mandible!" Danny glared.

"Does that mean you're refusing to tell us?" said McCord.

"I was here at home working out in the yard," Danny huffed.

"Can anyone corroborate that? Your neighbors, perhaps?"

"I was working in the backyard," Danny shook his head, "So, nope."

"Did you leave the house at all?" asked Buchanan.

"I took a break from the yard work and strolled along the waterfront."

"What time was that?"

"I don't know; early afternoon I suppose," Danny replied. Something dawned on him, "Did you look for any other guys named Dan Vogel?"

"We were given the name of Danny Vogel who was part of the Peninsula Theatre Group," McCord replied, "And you are the only one who fits that category."

"In other words," Buchanan added, "We're following wherever the leads take us."

"Well, your leads are taking you on a wild goose chase," responded Danny.

"In that case," said McCord, I'm sure you won't mind me taking your picture?"

"For what purpose?"

"To see if the proprietors of Walker Ranch recognize you."

"Fine… click away."

31

July 26th

"So I was thinking..." said Buchanan as he sat at his desk and contemplated the Officers' next move.

"Don't do that," interrupted McCord, "You'll give yourself a headache," he winked.

"We've got a comedian in the house this early in the morning?" Buchanan looked at this watch.

McCord showed off his pearly-whites.

"Anyway..." Buchanan paused to see if McCord was going to interrupt once again, "I was *thinking* that Mrs. Walker is going to be disappointed that there's no Samson & Delilah performance coming up after all."

"I'm thinking *that* news is going to sit a lot better than finding out a mandible she sold might be a murder weapon," responded McCord.

"You're planning on sharing that news when we go over there and show them the photo of Vogel?"

"Better for them to get it from us than seeing a report on the news, putting two-and-two together, and thinking that we're hiding something from them."

"Even though we have no proof that their mandible is the murder weapon?"

"I plan on sharing that detail with them as well," said McCord, "Perhaps that will allay some concerns?"

"Or have them sitting on pins and needles until the murder is solved," said Buchanan, "And worst-case-scenario at that point would be the killer confirming that he used their mandible to bludgeon the guy."

"Talk about a potential no-win situation for the two of them," McCord sighed as he grabbed his cell phone, scrolled through the contacts, and hit 'Send'.

"Who you callin'?" asked Buchanan.

"Detective Nash to give her a status report."

"Detective Nash..." echoed through McCord's phone.

"Detective; this is Officer McCord calling to give you an update on a few things Officer Buchanan and I have learned in regard to your case," stated McCord.

"Sounds good; what've you got?" the Detective replied.

"We found a local ranch here who sold a mandible to a gentleman the day before the murder," replied McCord, "They even provided us a name."

"That's great!"

"That's what we thought as well," said McCord, "But when we talked to the gentleman he said he never made such a purchase, so our next step is to bring a photograph of the guy back to the sellers of the mandible to see if they can positively identify him as the buyer."

"So, if I'm reading you correctly, the sellers will either make a positive identification," said the Detective, "Or the buyer purposely misled the couple by providing a false name?"

"That's correct; which in my mind could lean a couple of different directions," said McCord, "For one: If they I.D. this guy then he lied to us about the purchase, which certainly puts him in the crosshairs for the murder, especially since he has no alibi for that time frame. And for two: If he is *not* the buyer, then the *real* buyer set him up. And if the buyer is setting someone up there has to be a reason for it; like using the mandible in the commission of a crime for example. It also means the guy who got framed might be able to give us a name." McCord thought for a moment and added, "I guess what I'm saying is that this guy might be able to provide us a lead whether he's the guilty party or not."

"Some excellent deduction there," the Detective replied. "You'll give me an update after you show the photograph to the couple so we can determine our next step?"

"Of course."

"Great," replied the Detective. "If Officer Buchanan is there how about putting me on the speaker and I'll fill you both in on the Seabeck murder?"

McCord held up his phone in the direction of Buchanan and whispered "Seabeck murder update." He then commented into the phone, "Okay, you're on the speaker."

"The name of the victim is Michael Burke, age forty-seven," said the Detective. "As stated earlier, he was found face-down in some mudflats. He died from asphyxia, which was ruled to be a homicide as his head had been forcibly pushed down and held in the mud."

"How did you determine that about his head?"

"His face was literally halfway buried in the mud, almost leaving the imprint of a death-mask."

"Any forensic evidence?" asked Buchanan.

"Unfortunately, the tide had come in and washed over him," replied the Detective, "So if there was any evidence left by the perp, it had been washed away."

"Do you think the killer had stalked him and the rising tide was a planned forensic countermeasure?" said McCord, "Or are we looking at another stroke of bad luck - like the Paget scene with a flurry of yard sale folks trampling over evidence?"

"Could go either way on that one," replied the Detective, "The vic was one of those people who posted *every single movement he made* on social media; identifying his activity and exact location virtually hour-by-hour, minute-by-minute."

"So someone could have known his real-time location, and thus could have waited until he was in a remote area and then pounced?"

"That's entirely possible."

"Any persons of interest... possible motives?" said Buchanan.

"We're still looking into the guy's background, friends, possible enemies... you name it," replied the Detective.

"Understood," Buchanan replied.

"Earlier you said the vic also had a head wound," McCord directed to the Detective.

"That's correct," the Detective replied, "But we're somewhat on the fence on that one."

"Why is that?"

"We originally thought it was merely due to falling on rocks within the mud flats," said the Detective, "But now we think he could have been hit on the head with the rock, which knocked him down, possibly even knocking him out... and then he was asphyxiated."

"Makes sense," said McCord.

"Anyway, that's where we are at the moment," said the Detective.

"Thanks, Detective... we'll keep in touch."

"Roger that."

McCord hung up the phone.

Buchanan turned to McCord, "It sounds like the Detective is appreciative of our help."

"I suppose," McCord sighed, "Even though we haven't really given her any answers, just more questions."

"You're not feeling optimistic about the mandible?"

"The coincidental nature of such an odd sale occurring *right before* the same type of weapon was used in a murder is interesting, that's for sure," McCord replied, "But there's likely no way to tell for sure that the Walker's mandible is the same one used in the murder."

"Remember that the Detective said there were slivers of leather embedded in the mandible," said Buchanan, "So if the couple identifies Danny Vogel as the buyer, then it seems we should be able to get a search warrant, and perhaps find the gloves tied to the mandible?"

"You've got a point there," McCord nodded.

"On a separate subject," said Buchanan, "what do you make of the Seabeck murder?"

"It sounds like the evidence, or lack thereof, is going to be problematic."

"That's true," replied Buchanan. He paused in thought, "I can't get the visual of a death-mask out of my head."

"Yeah, that's a creepy one," McCord replied. He looked at his watch, "Let's go pay a visit to Henry and Phyllis Walker, shall we?"

- ❋ -

Rap-rap-rap McCord knocked on the door of the Walker residence. Henry Walker opened the door; Phyllis standing next to him. "Officers," Henry acknowledged.

"Good morning," McCord responded. "We talked to Danny Vogel; the gentleman who's a member of the Peninsula Theatre Group," he said and then handed his cell phone photograph to Henry, "Would this be the guy you sold the mandible to?"

Henry shook his head in a negative manner and handed the photo to Phyllis. "No, that's not him," they responded in unison as Phyllis returned the phone to McCord. "He was younger... mid-twenties maybe?" said Phyllis. "Dark curly hair, physically fit, about five-ten to six feet," added Henry.

"I was afraid of that," replied McCord.

"How's that?" said Henry.

"The gentleman, Danny Vogel, stated that he did not make the purchase," said McCord, "and he had no idea who would've used his name, or why they would have done so."

"Which means we are back to square one on this particular item," Buchanan added.

"And what, may I ask, is the issue?" Henry prompted.

"I'm not sure if you've read the paper or seen the news about a murder in Kitsap County last Sunday, but the murder weapon was an animal mandible," stated McCord, "Either from a donkey or a mule."

"Like ours," Phyllis grew wide-eyed.

"That's exactly the case, ma'am," McCord responded and then retrieved another photograph and held it up. "This is a picture of the mandible from the crime scene; I don't suppose there is any way that you can identify it?"

Phyllis grabbed the photo and shared it with Henry. After scanning it for several seconds Henry handed it back to McCord, "There was nothing unique about our particular mandible... they pretty much all look the same... I'm sorry we can't help you."

"I understand," said McCord as he placed the photo in his shirt pocket.

"Since the buyer lied and gave us a false name, I'm guessing he lied about the reason he wanted it?" asked Phyllis.

"I'm afraid so."

"If there's anything we can help with in the future, please let us know," said Henry.

"We will," McCord replied, "Thank you for your time."

McCord and Buchanan jumped in their cruiser and drove away.

"Well, that went pretty much as expected," McCord lamented.

"You know, I'm wondering if the guy who bought the mandible under a false name and pretense is also a part of the theatre group?" said Buchanan.

"And has a vendetta against Vogel?"

"Precisely."

"If he was trying to frame Vogel he wasn't very smart about it."

"Why do you say that?"

"You show your face to the sellers, you give them the name of a guy that looks nothing like you, a simple investigation discovers the inconsistency, and your attempted frame-job blows up in your face."

"I see what you mean," said Buchanan, "The actions of a novice for sure."

"Or not," said McCord as a notion hit him.

"Okay, you're just screwing with me, right?" responded Buchanan.

"Actually I'm not," McCord replied. "What if he formulated a plan to get hold of a mandible, but needed a viable reason when approaching a potential seller?"

"You're implying that he schemed the whole *'theatre group Samson & Delilah'* thing?"

"It would be the best way to ask about purchasing an animal mandible without drawing suspicion."

"Yeah, I see where you're coming from," Buchanan conceded. "But what would be the importance of an animal mandible in the first place? It makes no sense!"

"Good question," said McCord. "And I have no idea. But remember, it only has to make sense to the perp."

"That's not very comforting... trying to unearth a motive from nonsensical clues."

"Are you giving up on a potential future as a detective?"

Buchanan was surprised at the implication, "Says the guy who came across as being all lost and forlorn because we didn't provide any answers to the Detective, just more questions."

"Hey, we all have our moments," said McCord. "Besides, I've been reinvigorated."

"What was the impetus for that?"

"Beat me, but let's run with it before it wanes."

"Alright then," Buchanan replied. "On that note, your idea that the whole mention of a theatre group and associated play being a smokescreen got me to thinking."

"Let's hear it."

"Once the guy formulated his game-plan, maybe he just looked up the group's social media page, scrolled through the list of members, and picked Vogel to be his patsy?"

"I think you may be onto something."

"One of the many problems with everyone's crap being on social media," Buchanan shook his head at the current state of society. "People worry about identity theft, but I don't think they consider *this* manner of having one's identity taken."

"I agree," replied McCord, "Not stolen in the manner that is pervasive on the news... social security number, bank accounts, credit cards... but instead 'stolen'," he said with air-quotes, "to be used as a cover... a smokescreen... a frame-up."

"Exactly."

McCord looked at his watch, "What say we go talk to Swenson about what was seen by the joy-riding teenager out at Lookout Point?"

"I'm game."

32

Officers McCord and Buchanan stared at the door of Eric Swenson's apartment. "You go ahead," McCord said to Buchanan while nodding toward the door. "My pleasure," Buchanan replied.

Rap-rap-rap Buchanan pounded on the door.

Approaching footsteps could be heard on the other side of the door, then silence, then a not-so-muffled, "Son of a damn bitch!"

Buchanan turned to McCord, "Think we're getting under his skin?" he said.

"I'd say that's a safe assumption," McCord replied.

The apartment door slowly opened; Swenson glared at the Officers, but remained silent.

"Something wrong?" McCord directed to Swenson.

"No... why do you ask?" Swenson replied.

McCord nodded toward Buchanan, "We heard yelling," he stated.

"I just stubbed my toe," Swenson replied.

The Officers exchanged glances, and grins. "Alright then," said McCord.

"You know you guys are bordering on harassment," Swenson commented before McCord could speak. "What's the deal, you've got more 'Pearls of Wisdom'," he said with air-quotes, "that you want to blame on me?"

"Actually," Buchanan replied, "we received some new information regarding *certain activities* at Lookout Point when Caleb Rollins took his unfortunate tumble."

"Why do you guys keep trying to implicate me in a murder that never happened?" Swenson huffed. "This is how my tax dollars are spent? Why aren't you out pounding the pavement, walking your beat, whatever the hell they call it?"

McCord and Buchanan remained silent while awaiting the cessation of Swenson's venting.

Swenson's curiosity finally got the best of him; he crossed his arms and glared, "Fine; what's this *all new information* you are so eager to share?"

"How about I set the scene?" said McCord, who then proceeded to do so without allowing Swenson the opportunity to respond. "You rode your bicycle to the bridge and Lookout Point that day, correct?"

"Nice try," Swenson scowled, "Just to the bridge."

"Right," McCord replied. "And you were in the vicinity around the timeframe that Rollins fell to his death."

"So you say."

"A witness has come forward that saw two people arguing near the railing at that time."

"Yeah? So?"

"So one minute they're arguing, and the next minute... **poof**... Rollins has disappeared and only the guy with his bicycle is left."

"Yeah? And maybe all you've got is a *witness* to the guy taking a misstep and falling," said Swenson, "and they haven't come forward because they don't want to get railroaded like you're trying to do to me?"

"Perhaps; but somehow I'm thinking that's not the case" McCord replied and then attempted to throw Swenson off-kilter. "What did you do with your bicycle?"

"What are you talking about?"

"Heather said you were on-foot when she bumped into you on the bridge," McCord stated, "So I'm thinking you must have locked up your bicycle in the bike racks at Lookout Point."

"You're trying to trip me up and get me to admit I was at Lookout

Point?"

"I'm just trying to connect the dots... to get to the truth."

"I locked it up near the head of the bridge."

"That's an odd spot to park and lock your bike."

"Whatever."

"Okay then," responded McCord. "Oh; one more thing..."

"Now what?"

"The fact that Rollins grew up in your neighborhood and, more importantly, made inflammatory comments against you regarding your event on the bridge," McCord noted. "Then you have the responses to *his* comments that seemingly foretold his demise. And *then* you throw in the fact that *those* responses were eerily similar to your poetic writings." He paused to let the statement sink in and then added, "You see where I'm going with all this?"

"If you think I'm some nefarious killer why did you bother trying to save me on the bridge; why not just let me jump?" Swenson replied. "You see the irony in all this, right? You risk your life trying to save me, and you spend *every day since then* trying to convict me of a non-existent crime," he shook his head... "Ridiculous!"

McCord stood in quiet contemplation. Swenson had grown weary of the entire exchange, "Are we done?" he said.

McCord looked to Buchanan; who shrugged. McCord looked back to Swenson, "What do you know about donkey mandibles?" he blurted out.

Buchanan was caught off-guard by his partner's question, but not nearly as much as the person to whom it was directed...

"Wha... what??" Swenson stammered a reply.

"Oh, nothing," said McCord. "Enjoy the rest of your day."

Swenson shook his head and shut the door.

Once the Officers had reached their cruiser Buchanan turned to McCord, "What was the mandible question all about? You don't know something that *I* don't, do you?"

"Nah, I just wanted to see his reaction… throw him a curveball."

"Well it apparently worked; he had a major W-T-F look on his face," Buchanan grinned as he climbed into the driver's seat.

McCord slid into the passenger seat; he seemed to be in a momentary fog.

"Thinking up another curveball to throw at him?" Buchanan directed to McCord.

"Just re-running all of our conversations with him through my head," replied McCord, "There's something gnawing at me, but I'm not sure what it is."

"That sixth sense of yours, eh?"

McCord didn't respond; he was lost in thought.

33

His nerves were rattled as he slowly trod down the hallway. He had been overcome by a myriad of thoughts, ideas, questions, and eventual outcomes as he ran numerous scenarios through his head. He was looking for answers; but as each possible path was explored, no matter the far-reaching tangent, they all converged at the same endpoint. It was an endeavor steeped in frustration. What he had failed to realize was the difficulty of attempting to consider varying options when a single mind controls the narrative.

He entered the kitchen. In one fluid motion he opened the refrigerator door, grabbed a bottle of beer, and nudged the door shut with his elbow. He set the bottle on the counter, opened a cabinet drawer, retrieved a bottle opener, popped the cap off of the beer, and took several large gulps. He took a breath and wiped his mouth with his forearm, then scooted the bottle opener into the drawer and slid the drawer shut. He took another gulp.

He stared off into space; contemplating the situation. His mind wandered – a mixture of confusion and concern. He glanced around the area, seeking something... anything... that might point the way; a blank television screen in the living room drew him in.

Plopping down into the recliner he grabbed the remote and aimed it at the screen. As a picture emerged it was if fate had guided him to this moment in time. Reporter Danielle Stevenson was holding a microphone; behind her stood a sea of tall reeds.

"It was three days ago, Monday July twenty-third, in the north end of Kitsap County between Poulsbo and Kingston; that the body of Jared Paget was found in the marsh here behind me," Danielle nodded as she spoke into the news camera. "The location is just down the street from his home. Was he attacked while out for a stroll? Was he killed at home and his body dumped here in an attempt to delay its discovery? Questions whose answers are not yet known."

"Being an ongoing investigation, local law enforcement officials are withholding certain details surrounding the case. However, we do have a few facts to share," Danielle continued.

"Mister Paget held a yard sale over the weekend and several comments posted on social media regarding the sale were rather unflattering – some of them downright inflammatory. Thus, one theory is that the killer might have been a disgruntled customer. According to authorities, those persons who made the comments have been interviewed. None of them are currently identified as suspects, nor have any of them been officially ruled out.

"Another theory is that a customer desired an item that was not for sale, an argument ensued which turned into a physical altercation, resulting in the victim's death.

"A third possibility is that the killing is unrelated to the yard sale with exception that the numerous patrons and vehicles attracted by the sale could have provided the killer an opportunity to stalk their prey without drawing suspicion. This would also tend to imply that the victim knew his killer.

"Specific details of the investigation remain unclear as Kitsap County Sheriff's Department personnel and the Coroner's Office are keeping tight-lipped regarding both the cause of death and the associated murder weapon. However, unconfirmed reports point to an animal mandible of an unknown type as the potential implement of death. There are also unconfirmed reports that the weapon did *not* originate from the scene, but instead may have originated from a ranch in the Gig Harbor area."

His eyes grew wide. "What the f…" he started as he fumbled around to find the remote.

"When we return later in the newscast," Reporter Danielle stated, "we will provide an update to another murder..."

Remote finally in-hand, he clicked *off* the television before the reporter finished. His heart raced, his breaths grew large and deep – the remote slipped through his trembling hands. He scrambled to his feet and bolted out of the room.

34

July 27th

"Still grappling with our conversations with Swenson?" Buchanan directed to McCord as they sat at their respective desks.

"Admittedly... yes," McCord replied. "But something else dawned on me."

"About Swenson?"

"Not specifically; but in a sense... yep."

"Okay, you're sounding all mysterious."

"All three of these deaths... Rollins, Paget, and Burke... share a common denominator of sorts," noted McCord.

Buchanan's face scrunched-up. "Alright, you've got me," he said, "because I'm not seeing it."

"Social media."

"Social media?" Buchanan wondered.

"The commonalities are minimal; and definitely not a direct *'Cause & Effect'*," McCord replied, "But social media played a role in one manner or another in each case."

"You're going to have to enlighten me, because I'm still not seeing it."

"Take Rollins for starters," McCord said, "The whole exchange between him and the 'Pearl of Wisdom' character seeming to portend his demise."

"Okay; I'll grant you that one."

"Then with Paget; he advertised his yard sale on social media, which leads us to a few possibilities related to his death. *One:* There were disgruntled customers slamming the sale on his post, so one of them could be the killer. *Two:* The yard sale could have provided a killer both the location of his home, and a cover for being in the area... blending in with the crowd of potential buyers."

Buchanan nodded; he was starting to see where McCord was going with this line of thinking.

"And with Burke," McCord continued, "Someone could have stalked him and used his real-time locations that he posted on social media as an opportunity to pounce."

"Another one I just thought of," McCord added, "The ruse regarding the purchase of the mandible..."

"How's that?" Buchanan interrupted.

"We don't know how Vogel came to be the intended patsy, but it's possible that he was randomly selected from the theatre group's social media page."

Buchanan nodded.

"And even with Swenson; look at all the negative posts he received," McCord noted. "*Who knows* if the avalanche of ridicule will eventually push him over the edge?"

"So basically you're saying that social media is an evil entity that can destroy the very fabric of human decency," Buchanan commented.

McCord grinned, "Well I wouldn't go that far. But to borrow one of Swenson's descriptors, there *are* nefarious individuals online looking to cheat, steal, bully, and otherwise wreak havoc upon both the *lives*, and the *livelihood*, of others."

"You've got a point there," Buchanan sighed.

"Well I'll be go to hell..." McCord had an epiphany.

"What's that?"

"Something that Swenson said," McCord replied.

"The use of the term *nefarious?*" Buchanan responded.

"No; asking us if we had more *'Pearls of Wisdom'* to blame on him."

Buchanan connected the dots: "Shit, we hadn't thought to look for more posts and comments attributed to 'Pearl of Wisdom'," he said.

"Not any that might exist beyond the exchanges between this 'Pearl' character and Rollins."

"Damn straight!" McCord responded, "Let's go back through those posts and see what, if any, Pearls of Wisdom show up."

"On it!" Buchanan began to type, scroll, and click via his keyboard and mouse.

"Where are you starting?" said McCord.

"The same posting about the bridge event where I found the exchange with Rollin' Thunder," Buchanan replied.

"Okay; I'll check some of the news sites," McCord began to type.

Buchanan was mumbling out loud as he searched, "Nothing," he'd scroll, "Nothing," he'd scroll some more, "Nothing."

McCord was tempted to tell Buchanan that he could do without the play-by-play, but decided to let it slide.

"Ho-lee crap!" Buchanan suddenly blurted out.

McCord's head jerked in Buchanan's direction, "Whadda ya got?"

"You're not gonna believe it."

McCord stopped his search and darted over to Buchanan's desk.

"There's a frickin' exchange between 'Pearl of Wisdom' and Jared Paget," Buchanan pointed at his monitor.

"What the hell?" McCord replied as he saw the exchange. It read…

Paget: *"What a weak, pathetic, ass… an embarrassment to us REAL men. Men are supposed to be a pillar of strength, not some lame-assed pussy. What happened to your manhood, did your 'Delilah' lop it off?"*

Pearl of Wisdom: *"You mock one as a weakling, No Samson in your mind; Beware a Biblical reference, of whom ye have maligned; Lest reflection in the mirror, a Philistine thee find."*

"Doesn't the story go that Samson massacred and army of Philistines with the jawbone of an ass?" Buchanan relayed to McCord.

"You got that right," McCord replied. "If this isn't evidence that this Pearl of Wisdom character has some involvement in Jared Paget's murder I don't know what is."

"But it's only circumstantial at best," said Buchanan.

"I think you're looking at it from the perspective of having nothing more than a verbal exchange foretelling the circumstances surrounding a crime," McCord replied.

"Well, sure… because that's all we have."

"Right now that's true," said McCord, "But look at it this way: once you have a name you can hone in on that person, their activities, potentially place them at the scene, perhaps discover DNA, blood, fingerprints, you name it."

"Are we thinking Swenson?"

"You know my thoughts about him; but we can't go after him again with nothing more than the same line of conjecture we've already thrown at him," McCord replied, "or we really *are* looking at potential harassment charges."

"Then how do we get from here to there?"

"Barring some earth-shattering development we're at an impasse regarding Swenson," replied McCord, "But we definitely have a path forward."

"What's that?"

"Getting the Cyber Unit to determine the identity of this 'Pearl of Wisdom' character."

"Sounds good," Buchanan replied, "I'll get this stuff to the Captain, pronto."

"Not quite yet," McCord responded.

"Why not?"

"We stopped looking into Pearl of Wisdom when we found the exchange between him and Rollins," replied McCord, "and now we're discovering something that might have been useful days ago if we'd kept digging."

"Ahh…" Buchanan nodded, "We should continue to follow this thread until we've exhausted all options, and *then* take it to the Captain for her to forward on to the Cyber Unit?"

"Essentially... yes. Although I'm thinking what we've discovered is actually in Detective Nash's wheelhouse... since we're talking about Jared Paget's death."

"Makes sense," Buchanan said as recommenced his search, "I'm back on the trail."

"Sounds good," said McCord, "And I'll join you as soon as I fill up my coffee mug... we could be here awhile."

"Roger that."

McCord made his way to the Break Room to collect a fresh cup of brew, along with his thoughts. He couldn't shake the notion of what was, in his eyes, blatantly obvious: The disparaging, bullying, shaming remarks directed at Eric Swenson on social media, and the associated responses to those remarks that appear to portend each bully's demise. *"Could Swenson truly be behind the deaths of Rollins and Paget? Could he have a partner in these deeds? Could there be an unrelated vigilante exacting their own brand of justice who has no relation to Swenson whatsoever? Or am I jumping to conclusions... seeing something that does not actually exist?"* McCord thought to himself.

McCord filled up his coffee mug, took a sip, and ventured back toward his desk. "Any luck thus far?" he relayed to Buchanan as he approached.

"I'd say ho-lee crap again, but that would be redundant," Buchanan replied.

"No way," McCord responded as he decided to forgo his own desk and take a gander at Buchanan's monitor.

"I almost missed this one because it doesn't rhyme," Buchanan pointed at his screen.

"Another Pearl of Wisdom?"

"Yep; and guess who the exchange is with?"

"Umm... Danny Vogel?"

"No; we're talking *major W-T-F* territory," Buchanan replied, "Michael Burke."

"The vic in Seabeck? Are you frickin' kidding me?!"

"Here's the exchange," Buchanan replied, "Burke says: *"I don't understand why everyone is feeling sorry for this loser. 'Oh woe is me'; 'Cry me a river'. Either grow some stones, or make another attempt to jump... and be sure to put us all out of your misery and get it right this time"."*

"In reference to Swenson and the event at the bridge?" said McCord.

"Yep. And then Pearl of Wisdom responds: *"The slinger of mud, the thrower of stones; don't hold your breath. Actually, I guess you should, or should I say... will. Karma's a bitch when your words come back to haunt you"."*

"Karma's a bitch alright," McCord replied, "Hit in the head with a rock; and then smothered in the mud."

"Yeah," Buchanan replied, "I'm surprised he didn't mention a death-mask."

"I don't think that was an intended result," said McCord, "Otherwise I'm sure he'd be celebrating it."

"Think we've got enough now?" Buchanan pressed McCord.

"Definitely," McCord replied. "I'll get on the horn with Detective Nash and then we can update the Captain."

"Sounds good," Buchanan responded. "Whoa, I just thought of something," he added, "In light of this new info about Pearl of Wisdom, and our suspicions about Swenson, we should show his photo to the Walkers."

"I like the way you think," McCord pointed at Buchanan.

35

"I apologize if I sound overly optimistic or overly dramatic," McCord relayed over the phone to Detective Nash, "but Officer Buchanan and I have uncovered something that we believe could break your case wide open… potentially *both* of them."

The Detective was admittedly skeptical, yet also curious, regarding Officer McCord's proclamation. "Really?" she replied, "Let's hear it."

McCord relayed what Buchanan and he had unearthed concerning posts by an unknown 'Pearl of Wisdom' and his or her verbal sparring with both Jared Paget and Michael Burke.

The Detective was intrigued at the notion of a connection; particularly in regard to the similarities between Pearl of Wisdom's statements, and the manner of death of the victims. "Exactly how did you uncover this?" asked the Detective.

"As you know," McCord replied, "We were looking into the death of Caleb Rollins before it was officially ruled to be an accident, and we discovered this Pearl of Wisdom character going jab-for-jab with Rollins."

"Are you telling me that there's a heated exchange between this 'Pearl' guy and Caleb Rollins that mirrors those with Paget and Burke?"

"That's correct," said McCord, "And I may be reading more into the exchanges than is truly there; but from my perspective the verbiage appears to portend Rollins' death, just like those with Paget and Burke."

"Holy…" the Detective started, "Talk about a potential game-changer."

"Yes ma'am."

"Have you identified this person?"

"Unfortunately; no," replied McCord, "They've managed to hide their identity, and we don't have the technical ability to trace the source from our office. We were hoping…"

The Detective inadvertently cut McCord off, "Send me the links and I'll get our Cyber Team on it, ASAP."

McCord looked directly at Buchanan, "Officer Buchanan can get that to you post haste," McCord relayed to the Detective.

Buchanan gave McCord a thumbs-up concurrence with his statement to the Detective.

"Here's another piece of potentially relevant information about the posts," McCord continued, "The exchanges with both Rollins and Paget follow *Eric Swenson's* signature… in our opinion anyway."

"Eric Swenson?" the Detective was somewhat befuddled, "The guy you saved from jumping off of the Narrows Bridge?"

"That's correct," replied McCord. "I won't take up your time going over all of the details, but he tends to leave messages in rhyme… just like the Pearl character in both Rollins' and Paget's post. Another item of note is that his grandmother's name is Pearl."

"Whoa," the Detective replied, "So you're thinking Eric Swenson could be the source of these posts?"

"Hard to say for sure," McCord replied. "And I realize I could be way off-base here, but the similarities have been gnawing at me like there's no tomorrow. We did question him about the exchange with Rollins, but he pleaded ignorance. Also, as near as we can tell he has no alibi for the timeframes of Paget's and Burke's deaths, but to be honest we haven't pulled the string on that."

"Do you have any information as to what, if any, ties he might have to Paget or Burke? Whether or not he knows them?"

"Not at this time since he was only on our radar screen regarding Caleb Rollins, whom we *have* tied him to."

"Understood," the Detective stated as she tried to process everything. "Nonetheless, it looks like you might be onto something. If we run into any roadblocks trying to determine the identity of this Pearl of Wisdom character I might need you to send me everything you have on Swenson's rhymes, but don't worry about delving any more into that for the time being."

"Got it," McCord replied. "We also might be getting some additional info on Swenson within the next half-hour or so."

"In what manner?" the Detective wondered.

"We're taking his photograph to the sellers of the donkey mandible to see if they can identify him as the buyer."

"Great work," replied the Detective, "Anything else?"

"Not at this time."

"In that case I have an update for you two," replied the Detective. "Something the Coroner discovered about the Michael Burke murder: bruising on the back of his head and upper back. They are minor imprints… two partials, but they're indicative of what would be a waffle tread from a boot… a portion of the heel on his upper back, the ball of the foot on his head."

"So that's how he was suffocated?"

"That's the Coroner's opinion."

"I appreciate the update."

"No problem," replied the Detective, "Keep me posted; and I'll do the same."

"Yes, ma'am," McCord replied and then hung up the phone.

Buchanan looked toward McCord, "That would be great if the Detective's team can unearth the identity of this Pearl guy."

"No shit," McCord replied. "And it will be a MAJOR Ho-lee Crap moment if it turns out to be Swenson."

"That would be somethin', wouldn't it?" said Buchanan. "By the way, I just sent off the links to the Detective," he added as he leaned back in his chair.

"No time to relax," noted McCord, "Let's get over to the Walker's place."

36

"That's him... that's the guy!" Henry Walker pointed at the photograph of Eric Swenson.

"You're sure?" McCord replied as he continued to hold the photograph in front of Henry and Phyllis.

"Absolutely," Phyllis interjected.

There was a moment of silence as Henry, Phyllis, McCord, and Buchanan all exchanged glances; each of them trying to come to grips with the information.

Phyllis broke the silence. "Does this mean that our mandible was used in the commission of a crime?" she wondered.

"To be honest, ma'am," McCord replied, "We don't really know at this point."

Phyllis sighed as she pondered the possibilities.

The Officers glanced at each other and then back to Henry and Phyllis. "Well, that was all we needed right now," McCord extended his hand to the couple, "Thank you very much for your time."

"We're happy to have helped," Henry replied as Phyllis and he exchanged handshakes with the Officers.

McCord and Buchanan turned and walked away; Henry and Phyllis shut the door once the Officers had climbed into their cruiser.

Buchanan placed the key in the ignition and then turned to McCord. "No wonder Swenson had a major W-T-F look on his face when you asked him about a donkey mandible," he said.

"Yeah," McCord replied. He paused in thought. His demeanor was somewhat subdued as he attempted to wrap his head around the news. *"Could Swenson truly have murdered Jared Paget? What would drive him to such an act? Some idiotic post on social media? Who the hell does that?!"* McCord thought to himself.

"You know... your instincts about Swenson have been spot-on," Buchanan interrupted McCord's train of thought, "I don't know how you do it."

"I appreciate that, but don't give me too much credit," McCord replied, "we've got a lot of mystery yet to unravel."

"Not just us, but even more so, Detective Nash," noted Buchanan.

"That's true," McCord grabbed his cell phone. "We need to call her," he said as he scrolled through his contacts and hit 'Send'.

Detective Nash recognized McCord's number, "Officer McCord," she said as she answered her phone, "You have an update, I assume?"

"That's correct," replied McCord, "Henry and Phyllis Walker just positively identified Eric Swenson as the buyer of the mandible."

"To be honest," the Detective replied, "before you talked to me an hour ago I would not have seen that coming."

"Obviously we have no direct evidence to tie the mandible used in Paget's murder to the one allegedly purchased by Swenson," McCord stated, "but the circumstances are extremely curious at the very least."

"I think you have to add the caveat 'yet' to that statement," responded the Detective. "Remember that there were slivers of leather imbedded in the mandible, apparently from a pair of gloves; so if we find a pair we'll be looking for a forensic match. And if the sellers still have the animal's carcass on-site the lab may be able to match the mandible to those remains."

"I hadn't thought of that," McCord replied. "But hey, if we find gloves or any other potentially incriminating evidence I'll let you know," he added, "since he's the next item on the menu."

"Swenson?"

"That's correct."

"Be sure to proceed with caution; he may have an inclination that you're on to him," replied the Detective, "And you have no idea how dangerous a wild animal can be when they feel threatened."

"Understood."

"Keep me posted."

"I will," McCord replied and hung up the phone.

Buchanan started the car. "Next stop Swenson's?" he said.

McCord gave Buchanan the thumbs-up; Buchanan hit the gas.

"I wonder if Swenson has an alibi for the Kitsap murders?" Buchanan said as he and McCord headed toward Eric Swenson's apartment.

"Murders? As in *plural...*" McCord replied, "You're implicating him in the Seabeck murder as well?"

"No one else is on the radar screen for that murder, so I figure it can't hurt to look."

"I don't disagree, but let's not show our hand on that one when we talk to him, let's focus on the mandible," McCord replied, "and the fact that he was all beat to hell when we saw him Sunday... possibly due to an altercation with Paget."

"Good point," Buchanan replied. "We know he won't be able to use *work* as an alibi since he hasn't been back following the incident on the bridge."

"We also know that we *can* tie him to the timeframe of Rollins' fall," said McCord, "But I think we need to steer clear of revisiting that issue right now."

"Something just hit me that could be problematic," said Buchanan.

"What's that?"

"You don't think Heather would provide him an alibi in order to cover for him, do you?"

"Whew, that's a tough one," McCord replied. "Hard to imagine she would lie for him."

"Yeah, but how often do we see people who are in complete denial when it comes to a loved one?" Buchanan responded, "They are so sure that the person couldn't be guilty of a crime that they will say almost anything to protect them?"

McCord's cell phone rang. He looked at the Caller I.D. "Whoa, speak of the devil," he said. "Officer McCord," he stated as he answered the phone.

"Officer, it's Heather Kincaid," Heather replied.

"Yes, what can we do for you?" McCord replied.

"It's about Eric; he just called and was talking crazy stuff... like running away together and eloping."

"I take it that you've had no discussions about trying to work things out?"

"Quite the opposite," Heather replied. "First of all, our wedding was scheduled to take place *a year* from now, so eloping *now* would be way off-base even if things were normal. But worse than that, like I've been telling you, there is no more 'us'," she explained. "He has basically turned into a scary stalker-dude. I don't even recognize him anymore; he's lost all sense of reality. Who knows what his state of mind is at this point... what he's capable of?"

"Where are you right now?"

"I'm home, but I have a wedding rehearsal and dinner to attend later at the Chapel on Echo Bay."

"On Fox Island?"

"Yes."

"Okay; we'll track down Mister Swenson and have a chat with him," McCord replied. "If he contacts you or shows up, you need to call me right away."

"I will," Heather responded and hung up the phone.

McCord turned to Buchanan, "Did you happen to catch all that?"

"Yeah," said Buchanan, "And it sounds like maybe we don't have to worry about Heather covering for Swenson after all." He thought for a moment and added, "Although I don't know why you didn't tell her we were already on our way to talk to Swenson, and instead implied we'd be going there based on her request?"

"Better for her to think we're showing up on her account, and not because he's a person of interest in a murder."

"Otherwise she might feel the need to cover for him?" Buchanan wondered.

"Yep."

37

The Officers met Tanner Hughes, the apartment manager, at the top of the third floor stairs... about twenty feet from Eric Swenson's front door.

"Mister Hughes," McCord directed to Tanner, "Please remain here while we see if Mister Swenson is home. If he does not respond then we'll have you come over and unlock the door."

"I understand," Tanner replied.

The Officers walked over and positioned themselves at the door of Swenson's apartment. *Rap-rap-rap* McCord knocked – no response. "Eric Swenson; Officers McCord and Buchanan. We need a moment of your time," McCord stated loudly.

Not a peep.

McCord looked over to Tanner and gave him the 'come hither' finger-wave. Tanner complied.

Tanner unlocked the door. McCord gave him a directive, "Remain out here and do NOT enter the apartment unless we specifically request your presence."

"Yes Sir," Tanner replied.

The Officers drew their weapons. Tanner grew wide-eyed and slowly backed away to the comfort of the stairwell.

"Eric Swenson, we're coming in!" McCord yelled as Buchanan and he entered the apartment. Once again, there was no response.

As they approached the first doorway – the bedroom, McCord peeked in while Buchanan had his back. "Clear," McCord stated.

The Officers reversed the action at the next doorway – the bathroom; Buchanan entering while McCord had his back. "Clear," Buchanan stated.

The next stop was the laundry room. McCord peeked in; he noticed Swenson's bicycle hanging on hooks on the far end of the room. "Clear," he said. "Well, we know he's not out for a bike ride," he added.

The Officers repeated the sequence until they had gone through the entire apartment. They holstered their weapons.

"Well, now what?" said Buchanan.

"Let's scan the area to see if we can get an idea as to his location," McCord replied.

"And if we find more notes, poems, lyrics, whatever?"

"We assess and bag those suckers," said McCord, "They could provide us more clues."

"Roger that."

Unlike their first visit, no scraps of paper encapsulating the thoughts, ideas, and notions within Eric Swenson's mind were found.

When the Officers walked back past the laundry room something caught McCord's eye: A pair of gloves draped over the crossbar of the bicycle. "Gloves," he pointed out to Buchanan.

"And work boots," Buchanan pointed in a different direction, "Over there in the far corner of the room."

"Whoa," McCord responded as he spied the boots. He extracted, and began to don, a pair of latex gloves; Buchanan followed suit.

McCord proceeded to the gloves; Buchanan to the boots.

Grasping the gloves one-at-a-time off of the crossbar, McCord commented, "Leather... and pretty scratched-up," he said as he scanned them. "Hard to say if it's due to wielding a mandible as a weapon," he added. "Or from taking a tumble on his bike."

Buchanan grabbed a boot and flipped it over to eyeball the sole. "Muddy... with waffle treads," he commented.

"Just like the bruising on the Seabeck vic," McCord noted.

"Yep," Buchanan nodded as he looked over the second boot.

McCord stood in almost-stunned disbelief, *"It can't be... can it?"* he thought to himself.

Buchanan noticed McCord's contemplative demeanor, "Something on your mind?"

"Uh... nah," McCord reemerged from his fog. "Hey, can you go grab some evidence bags out of the cruiser while I call both our Forensic Team and Detective Nash?"

"Can do," Buchanan replied as he returned the boots to the floor and exited the apartment.

McCord extracted his cell phone, but almost dropped it as it buzzed before he could make his call – it was Detective Nash. "Detective," McCord spoke as he answered, "I was just about to call you."

"How fortuitous," replied the Detective, "You want to go first?"

"Go ahead."

"Our Cyber Team has unveiled the man behind the mask – it's Eric Swenson."

"Holy crap!"

"Yeah, your intuition was correct," the Detective replied, "Have you gotten to his place yet?"

"We're there now; which is what I was calling about," McCord replied. "Swenson is nowhere in sight, but we found a pair of muddy boots with waffle treads, and also a pair of gloves – we're getting ready to bag 'em and tag 'em," he added as Buchanan arrived and started bagging up evidence.

"Damn," the Detective started, "I did not expect that."

"Nor did we," McCord replied, "But now we need to find him before he extends his wrath to someone else."

"Once again... proceed with caution."

"We will," McCord replied. He suddenly had a disconcerting thought, "Crap; his ex-fiancé called about a half-hour ago and said he had called her and was acting like a whack-job."

"Do you know where she is?"

"She said she was at home."

"Then you'd better go."

"Yep," McCord replied as he hung up the phone and then immediately dialed Heather's number – her phone went directly to voicemail. "Shit!" McCord turned to Buchanan, "We need to get over to Heather's place."

38

He wheeled into the parking area of Donkey Creek Park and rolled to a stop. He was nearly hyperventilating; his hands shaking. *"Think man… think!"* he said to himself. He looked at his watch. He took a deep breath.

He glanced around the area; there was nary a soul in sight, only a couple of vehicles – one sitting twenty yards away, a second one parked at the far end of the lot. Both vehicles appeared to be empty. He glanced at the rear view mirror – nothing but a sea of trees, shrubs, and ferns sitting silent. He readjusted the mirror to catch a glimpse of the eye of the beholder. "What a wretched, worthless piece of shit," he said to himself aloud. He returned the mirror to its normal position.

Slipping his hand into his left pants pocket, he extracted his cell phone. He scrolled through the contacts and hit 'Send'. The line went directly to voice mail. "Dammit!" he said aloud. He immediately re-hit 'Send'. Once again the line went directly to voice mail. "Rrrrrr," he growled. He re-hit 'Send' – same response. He found himself being taunted by the voice mail message each time he repetitively hit 'Send'. His frustration grew while his patience waned. After a half-dozen attempts his patience disappeared. "DAMMMITTT!!" he screamed at the top of his lungs. He caught his breath and looked around to see if anyone had heard his exclamation of frustration.

He exited his car and began an intensely-focused journey from the park, to Harborview Drive, and toward the residential section of the harbor. Cell phone in hand, his pace alternated between a brisk walk and a jog, periodically interrupted by additional attempts to make contact via his phone.

He rounded a corner and stopped – Heather's house was in view. Her car was neither out front nor in the driveway, but that was not unusual as she often parked in the garage. He recommenced his trek while keeping his eyes peeled for her car or bicycle; or a more troubling sight – a police cruiser.

He stepped onto the landing, took a moment to scan the area, and pounded on the door. "Heather, it's Eric, we need to talk!"

No response.

Pound-pound-pound "Heather!!" he yelled.

Nothing.

He reached into his pocket, extracted a key, inserted it into the deadbolt slot, and unlocked the door. He opened the door and slithered inside. He shut and latched the door behind him.

"HEATHER!" he screamed.

He glanced around the living room, took a deep breath, and then began to dart around the house like a man possessed. "Heather!" he continued to yell as he searched. He poked his head into the bathroom – nothing. He stepped into the bedroom – once again... nothing. His frustration was building. He swung the door open between the kitchen and the garage – her car was gone. "Dammit!" he yelled as he slammed the door shut.

Having failed to catch Heather at home he now had a new objective: seeking-out clues to her whereabouts.

He returned to the bedroom and began to rummage through the space – nothing of note on the bed, or in the closet. He knelt down and looked under the bed. As he stood up something on the nightstand caught his eye – an open book with a card sitting atop the pages. He grabbed the card; it was an invitation to a Rehearsal Dinner at The Chapel on Echo Bay. He looked at his watch – the event was occurring in an hour-and-a-half. When he went to place the card back upon the book he noticed that it wasn't a book at all – it was a diary; and it was open to an entry dated July 20th.

His heart raced as he read the cries of despair within the page. Each sentence creating a fresh wound, cutting deeper and deeper as the story painted a portrait of a woman in anguish… a woman questioning herself and her decisions: past, present, and most pointedly, her future. His eyes welled-up when he read the last line. The words *'All I can think of is Raymond. I am overwhelmed with guilt'* ripped his heart wide open.

"This is a fate worse than death," he said to himself aloud while the tears began to flow, "I should have died that day."

He read the page again… and again. It was not solely the written words that were tearing at him, but what he was reading between the lines… words that existed only within his fertile, yet fragile, mind. The web you weave between reality and fantasy… the story you conjure from your own thoughts, dreams, and nightmares… can be a dangerous thing.

His demeanor began to change. The tears ceased; and his heartbreak turned first to anger, and then to rage. "What the hell *else* is in here?!" he snarled as he manipulated the upper corner of the page. He began to flip to the next page when he was startled by several knocks on the door. He dropped the diary.

"Ms. Kincaid, it's Officers McCord and Buchanan," rang out from the other side of the front door.

"*Shit!*" he said to himself.

He scurried over to the bedroom window and slid it open. He peeked out to the back yard; there was no one in sight. He listened for sounds of a gate unlatching, or of footsteps along the side yard gravel and stepping stones; there was nothing but silence.

Another knock on the door was his cue to scramble out the window. He landed in the yard, made a quick scan of his surroundings, and bolted across the property and over the fence. He blazed through a neighbor's yard, down the street, and zig-zagged from street to avenue to street to avenue until he had given himself a several-block buffer-zone from the police officers.

He crossed Harborview Drive and, instead of heading directly to Donkey Creek Park, he took a detour to Austin Estuary Park. He considered catching his breath and collecting his thoughts while within the confines of the park, but his adrenalin overruled such a notion, and he proceeded along the trail that runs between the two parks.

Having transitioned to a brisk yet methodical walk, he made his way to his car, climbed in, and sat there in a hyper-vigilant stupor. He took a deep breath. He was relieved that he had escaped a potential run-in with the cops, but he now had an all-new endgame in mind... courtesy of Heather's diary entry.

He started the car, backed out of the parking spot, and hit the gas.

39

Officers McCord and Buchanan stood on the porch of Heather Kincaid's home. They had knocked and yelled-out to Heather, but there was no response. They had also taken a peek through the front window into the living room; there was no activity within.

"What do you think?" Buchanan inquired of McCord, "We don't really have probable cause to bust open the door, do we?"

"That's a tough one," McCord replied. "Two things have me concerned: Heather not answering her cell phone; and the fact that we traced Swenson's cell phone GPS to the vicinity before he apparently turned off the phone or the GPS function."

"Yeah, but the *vicinity* was just Harborview Drive, not right here at Heather's house," Buchanan replied. "And Swenson's car is nowhere in sight."

"True," McCord sighed.

A hush of uncertainty overtook the moment as the Officers considered the situation... and their options.

Buchanan broke the silence, "This is frickin' crazy!" he began to vent. "I mean, we thought there might be something fishy about Rollins' death; you know... Swenson's potential involvement; but how the hell could Swenson have hunted-down and murdered both Paget and Burke?"

"The Detective is looking into both victims and whether Swenson knew either of them; but maybe he was trolling them on social media? After all, we now know that it was Swenson who exchanged verbal barbs with both of them online... barbs that seemed to foretell their deaths."

"You're saying that all the seemingly far-fetched stuff you postulated for each scenario could be more than mere speculation?"

"As mind-boggling as that sounds, it certainly looks possible," McCord shrugged. "But that's a mystery we can worry about deciphering once we catch him."

"Yeah, I guess," Buchanan moaned. "So now what?"

"Well hell, before we head back to the Station let's at least look through the windows and check out the yard."

The Officers decided to circle the house counter-clockwise, which took them to the gate on the right side of the garage. Opening the gate revealed a narrow side yard, with the garage window a few feet to the left. McCord glanced through the window, "No car in the garage," he stated.

The Officers resumed their trek. Now at the back of the house they came upon a sliding glass door. Buchanan took a peek. "Dining room," he said. "I can also see a portion of the kitchen," he added. "You can probably get a better view through that window," he pointed to his right.

McCord walked over and looked through the window. "Yep," he said. "Empty."

The Officers worked their way to the last window along the back of the house. "This sucker's wide open," McCord commented. He stuck his head in, "Bedroom," he stated.

"What do you think?" said Buchanan.

"There's a book lying on the floor near the bed and the nightstand... I'm not sure what to make of that," McCord replied. He intensified his focus and twisted his head to one side. "Actually, it looks like the cover says 'Diary'," he squinted.

"Whoa," Buchanan perked up, "If anything happens to Heather it could be a source of possible clues."

"Let's hope we don't have a reason to delve into her personal thoughts, hopes, and dreams," McCord sighed.

"Yeah," Buchanan breathed.

"Other than that nothing appears to be out of place, so maybe she just likes to leave her window open on a warm summer day?"

"Head back to the Station?"

"I guess so," McCord replied.

The Officers returned to their cruiser. After McCord slid into the passenger seat and buckled-up he made another call to Heather – her phone went directly to voicemail. "Damn," McCord stated as he hung up.

Buchanan started the car and headed down the road. "Still no luck, eh?" he said.

"Nope," McCord shook his head.

"And Swenson's GPS?"

McCord looked at the cruiser's laptop. "Still off," he exhaled.

It was a short drive to the Station. As the Officers entered they were immediately approached by the Sergeant. "You two need to get out to Fox Island; there's a reported disturbance at the Chapel on Echo Bay," he said.

"You've got to be shitting me!?" replied McCord as he started to head back out the door.

"What's up?" said Buchanan, right on McCord's heels.

"Heather said that she had a Rehearsal Dinner there this evening."

"You don't think...?" Buchanan started.

The Officers made a beeline to their cruiser, jumped in, and buckled up. McCord reached into his pocket and grabbed his cell phone. "What the hell?!" he stated as he stared at the screen.

"What is it?" Buchanan inquired.

"A missed call from Heather," McCord replied as he hit 'Send'. The line rang... and rang... and rang... until it went to voicemail.

"Crap!" McCord commented and then hit 'End call'.

40

Miranda had called the police as soon as she saw Eric Swenson exit his vehicle and commence yelling-out for Heather. The parents of the bride and groom had not yet arrived, nor had the groomsmen; and Miranda wanted to defuse the situation before things got out of hand. She had no idea how Swenson had tracked Heather down, but she knew there would be a potentially volatile confrontation based on everything Heather had shared with her.

The other members of the wedding party were surprised to see Swenson arrive as well. There was a level of unease… of angst among them; especially when Swenson began to rant.

Swenson walked into the chapel area. "Where's Heather?!" he growled to the group.

Everyone remained quiet.

"I know she's here!" Swenson yelled, "Her car's outside!" he thumb-pointed.

"Eric," Miranda stepped forward, "This is not the time or the place."

Swenson stuck his pointer finger in Miranda's face, "You stay out of this!"

Miranda stepped back.

"Heather!!" Swenson yelled.

Hearing Swenson's voice, and fearing for the well-being of her friends, Heather walked into the chapel area from an adjoining room. "Eric, what are you doing here?" she said.

"We need to talk," Swenson replied.

Heather head-nodded toward the room from which she had just entered.

"Heather," Miranda pleaded, "Don't."

"It's okay," Heather replied.

Swenson followed Heather into the room. He shut and locked the door.

"Why did you lock the door?" Heather asked.

"So we don't get interrupted before I'm finished... uh... before *we're* finished," replied Swenson.

Silence overtook the room. Heather wasn't sure what to say; Swenson was in a fog – breathing heavily and repetitively glancing between Heather and the floor.

"You wanted to talk?" Heather prodded while Swenson was staring at the floor.

Swenson looked back up at Heather, "My whole life has gone to hell."

"You're only twenty-five; you have an entire lifetime ahead of you."

"A week or two ago maybe... but not anymore," Swenson sighed.

"You can't think that way," Heather replied. "Things may seem bad now, but they'll get better."

"Better?? BETTER?? Are you kidding me?!!"

Heather flinched at Swenson's aggressive response; which only raised Swenson's ire; "Why did you jump back?! What... you're afraid I might do something crazy?!!"

"Come on Eric, let's discuss this calmly."

"Calmly?! After everything you've done to me I'm supposed to remain CALM?!"

"Things shouldn't have to end this way," Heather stated.

"End this way??!! That's all you've been wanting, isn't it... for things to end... for ME to end?!"

"That's not what I meant."

"That's a load of bull... I know more than you *think* I know!"

Heather was confused, "What are you talking about?"

"Oh, we'll get to that," Swenson replied, "but not just yet."

Heather stood silent, trying to grasp the meaning of Swenson's statement.

"You know, you almost got your wish the other day," Swenson nodded.

"My wish?? *What* wish?"

"I was going to jump off the bridge right in front of you."

"What??"

"But I caught you mid-span instead of near the suspension cables where I could climb to the top of the tower," Swenson explained. "The bridge itself would not be dramatic enough; but a *swan-dive off the top of the tower?* Now THAT's dramatic! That's what you wanted to see, didn't you?!"

Heather was horrified at the thought, "Of course not!"

"Plus, I had that bully to take care of," Swenson added – paying little attention to Heather's response.

"A bully?" Heather shook her head, "You're not making any sense."

"I told you all about those stupid bullies!" Swenson replied and then continued his rant, "Insensitive assholes bashing a guy who was in such despair he was ready to take his own life. They hide behind a façade on these social media sites, but it is *they* who are the TRUE cowards and deserve the pain they inflict on others to come right back at them... like a knife-edged boomerang." He paused in thought, "But hell... they aren't pointing and laughing anymore. Like the saying goes, '*he who laughs last, laughs best*'," he grinned.

Heather was beginning to comprehend Swenson's rant; and was growing concerned with the implication therein.

Swenson continued in an almost-hypnotic state... "I can only imagine what went through their heads as they tried to decipher my responses to their posts." He looked up at Heather, "You should have seen the look on their faces when I showed up," he lit up as he re-lived the moment. "Actually, it wasn't when I showed up, it was when the gates of Hell opened up and swallowed them... courtesy of my hand," he grinned and nodded with a sense of satisfaction.

Heather had a look of despair on her face, "What... what are you talking about?"

"I'm talking about KARMA!!"

Swenson extracted a .38 caliber revolver that had been tucked inside his pants and covered-up by his un-tucked shirt. He placed the barrel of the gun against his temple. "And that's what YOU wanted, isn't it? Karma! ...to get rid of me!"

"What are you doing?!" Heather replied in horror. "Of course that's NOT what I wanted! Now STOP... PLEASE!"

Swenson pointed the gun at Heather, "Don't tell me what to do!!" He then placed the barrel of the gun back on his temple.

Heather stepped back and placed her hands in a guarded position.

Bzzz-bzzz

"What the hell is that?!" Swenson yelled as he nodded toward the source of the buzzing sound.

"My cell phone," Heather replied, "in my purse here on the chair," she pointed.

"Grab it and hand it over," Swenson gestured with the gun.

Heather reached into her purse, extracted her cell phone, and handed it to Swenson while it continued to buzz.

Swenson looked at the caller I.D., "Officer McCord?! That fucking cop??!!" he glared at Heather as he pushed the phone in her face. He pulled the phone back and hit 'End call'.

❊❊❊

"Dammit!" Officer McCord said as he hung up his cell phone.

"Heather's cell went to voice mail again?" Officer Buchanan asked McCord as he sped along Warren Drive NW, almost to the Fox Island Bridge.

"Not this time," McCord replied. "Someone answered and then hung up."

"Shit; that doesn't sound good."

"Yeah," McCord sighed. "How far away are we?"

"Maybe five minutes."

❊❊❊

"You want the cops, do you?" Swenson said to Heather. "Okay, I can oblige," he dialed 9-1-1 and then returned the gun barrel to his temple while holding the phone with his other hand.

"9-1-1 Operator, what are you reporting?" echoed through the phone.

"A dead body," Swenson replied.

Heather tried to speak, but her voice was silenced by fear. She stumbled back into the chair.

"Do you know the identity of the victim?" asked the Operator.

"She's my fiancé."

"Are you sure she's dead?"

"She *will be* in a minute," Swenson pointed the gun at Heather, and then back to his temple. "Me too," he added, "But not quite yet."

The Operator was confused; she wasn't sure she heard Swenson correctly. "She *will* be??" the Operator questioned.

"Yeah," Swenson replied, "And tell Officer McCord that I said '*Thanks*'".

The Operator was now befuddled, "Tell Officer McCord '*Thanks*'??" she repeated Swenson's statement.

"For providing me this opportunity," Swenson clarified and then hung up.

A siren could be heard off in the distance.

"It sounds like your *Knight in Shining Armor* is trying to come to your rescue," Swenson nodded toward the window.

A tear rolled down Heather's cheek. "Eric... please..." she managed with a garbled voice.

The siren was getting louder.

"Once we're done here," Swenson said, "I'm going after Raymond."

"Raymond?" Heather replied, "Who's Raymond?"

"Don't play ignorant or innocent with me!" Swenson yelled as he aimed the gun at Heather. "I read that page in your diary… your entry last Friday, the 20th… *'All I can think of is Raymond'!"*

"It's not what you think!" Heather proclaimed as she reached into her purse.

"LIAR!!" Swenson screamed as he pulled the trigger.

Shrieks reverberated throughout the chapel at the sound of gunfire.

Swenson walked over to Heather's lifeless body. Lying between her purse and her hand was an invitation stamped SAMPLE. It read… *'Please help us celebrate the wedding of Eric Swenson and Heather Kincaid on Saturday, July 27th, 2019 at 2pm in the historic Raymond Inn in Raymond, Washington'.*

"NOOOOOO!" Swenson yelled. He put the barrel of the gun against his temple.

'BAM!!'

41

Officer McCord snapped back to reality from a trans-like state. Eric Swenson was dangling off of the bridge tower; one hand grasping a wire cable surrounding the tower, the other hand barely clinging to McCord's wrist.

"Hang on... I've got you," said McCord as he struggled to maintain his grip.

"Just let me go!" Swenson cried out as he let go of the cable wire.

McCord attempted to tighten his grip – hanging onto Swenson's wrist with every ounce of strength he had remaining; but would it be enough?

Swenson's grasp was weakening... almost nonexistent. McCord's grip was now the single thread keeping Swenson from certain death, and it was unraveling – his grip was mere seconds away from failing.

In a moment of clarity McCord pondered what could be... what *would* be. His grip failed him.

Swenson's eyes grew wide in shock, disbelief, horror as he began to fall. A blood-curdling shriek faded into the abyss as Swenson plunged to his death.

McCord flopped onto his stomach – exhausted. He took a moment to attempt to recover his strength before the long trek back down the suspension cable. He also needed that moment to take pause and reflect... to gather his thoughts... to regain his composure. His heart raced, his body trembled; his hands shook almost uncontrollably. As he was trying to make sense of it all... what he had just experienced... the gravity of moment; he was startled by an approaching sound. He turned around and stumbled to his feet - grabbing the cable wire to steady himself. There before him stood a Rescue Officer wearing a harness... two more harnesses draped over his shoulders.

McCord looked to the Officer, "I couldn't hold on," he exhaled.

"You did all you could," replied the Officer.

"Yeah, I guess you're right," McCord sighed. "His time was up; no matter the outcome," he shook his head.

"Are you implying that his fate was sealed?"

"That's one way to put it."

"What makes you say that?"

"Call it..." McCord paused in thought, "...a premonition."

Ronald Lamont

Gig Harbor Register – July 29th

FOX ISLAND – Gig Harbor residents Miranda and Colby Knudsen exchanged wedding vows at The Chapel on Echo Bay yesterday afternoon. The bride, the former Miranda Davis, is a 2009 graduate of Gig Harbor High School and a 2013 graduate of Western Washington University. The groom, Colby Knudsen, is a 2007 graduate of Peninsula High School and a 2012 graduate of Western Washington University.

The bride's best friend since grade school, Ms. Heather Kincaid, served as Maid of Honor. The groom's brother, Carl Knudsen, served as Best Man.

The Chapel on Echo Bay was also the site of the wedding reception. The reception included a remembrance of one of the original members of the wedding party, groomsman Eric Swenson, whom had tragically lost his life a week-and-a-half prior... falling to his death off of the Tacoma Narrows Bridge.

Ronald Lamont

Excerpt from

SMOKE AND MIRRORS

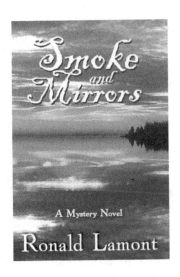

1

The anticipation was palpable - the rapid heartbeat, the cold sweat, the shortness of breath a gasp away from hyperventilating, the overwhelming feeling of... excitement. *"Revenge is a dish best served cold"* so the saying goes; how ironic that it was about to be served at a couple-thousand degrees. A flickering flame atop a matchstick buffeted by an early autumn breeze at one moment... a raging conflagration the next.

The point of no return passed hours ago; there was no turning back now. Various scenarios had been accounted for, anomalies assessed, course corrections made, and everything had fallen into place. Months of painstaking research, meticulous planning, setting the traps, covering your tracks - all converging at this particular place and time.

The midnight sky was pitch-black, save for a sliver of a crescent moon overhead. Off in the distance emanated the lights of the city, oblivious to the darkness of this deed.

Dead silence was interrupted by the sounds of nature - the rustling of leaves in the breeze… the trickle of a nearby stream.

A face suddenly appeared upon the reflection of the glass as the flame was lit – it was the face of vengeance… the face of evil.

A phone call was made just as the match ignited its means to an end.

A groggy, barely audible "Hello?" reverberated through the phone.

'Click' and the phone met its fate in the fledgling fire.

As the inferno began to spread a single act remained… get the hell out of there.

2

"Hey Nash, you've got a live one," said Sheriff Steven Clarke as Mackenzie Nash walked past his office on her way toward the aroma wafting through the space that was drawing her in – a freshly-brewed pot of coffee.

"A live one??" she replied as she grabbed the coffee pot and began to pour, stopping at half a cup – anticipating but a brief moment to enjoy her morning java.

"A figure of speech – SCFD responded to an early morning fire out near Blue Heron Cove."

"An apparent homicide?"

"That's their take; a body, along with indications of an accelerant. The Arson Team is on the way."

"If I'm getting the call I assume the Coroner or his Deputy is on the way as well," said Nash; stopping to take a sip of her coffee, "You got an address?"

"3756 Salmon Beach Road."

Nash took another sip, exhaled, and looked at her watch. She pondered the time of morning and grabbed her cell phone, "Hey Dirk, when you're done with your morning ritual meet me out near Blue Heron Cove – 3756 Salmon Beach Road to be specific."

Nash poked her head into Sheriff Clarke's office, "I left a message for Brogan; if he happens to show up here can you send him out to the scene?"

"Got ya covered."

Nash gulped down the last of her coffee, grabbed her gear, and headed out the door.

Mackenzie Nash is the Lead Detective in the Homicide Unit of the Slaughter County Sheriff's Department. She's as hard-nosed as they get – molded for this line of work at an early age. She grew up fast – not necessarily her choice; and never had a father-figure in her life as her parents divorced when she was six and 'Dear old Dad' was never to be seen again.

Being the eldest child she was always in something of a position of authority in the household; especially since her mother had to work two jobs just to make ends meet, thanks to the fact that when the XY chromosome disappeared anything resembling child support disappeared with him.

It didn't help that her mother apparently had no qualms about putting the burden of caring for the two youngest girls on Mackenzie's shoulders – routinely staying after her shift at the lounge to have a drink or two with the customers; and even worse, showing up at midnight with some *less than honorable* gentleman in tow.

When Mom remarried several years after her divorce Mackenzie thought things might change for the better, but it turned out that stepdad had no desire to be involved in the girls' lives – not in a good way at least.

One morning the two young girls confided in Big Sister that stepdad would sneak into their room late at night and "*just be creepy.*" It started with him standing near the end of the bed, watching them, for what seemed like an eternity to the poor girls even though it was only a few minutes. It wasn't long before he started sitting on the edge of the bed. They'd pretend they were asleep and pray he would go away. "Why isn't Mom stopping him from doing this??" they would whisper to each other.

One night, "*Mister Creepy*" started to slip his hand under the covers of the youngest child; she let out an "Aaah!" as if she had been asleep and was suddenly awakened by the touch of The Boogie Man. The Boogie Man bolted out of the room and the late night visits stopped for a while.

After that experience the girls tucked their blankets tightly under the mattress like a bunk in a military barracks. Better yet, Mackenzie set a trap – sprinkling little confetti-sized stars from the youngest girl's Glitter and Sparkle kit on the end of the bed.

When stepdad was caught strolling down the hallway in the middle of the night with the backside of his PJs covered in little stars the shit hit the fan – Mackenzie confronted him like a seasoned interrogator… a portent of her future career. Mom got a dressing-down as well for risking her kids at the hands of this scumbag. Stepdad was subsequently tossed out on his star-sprinkled ass, and the Nash family returned to normal, as it were.

Excerpt from

RISEN FROM THE DEPTHS

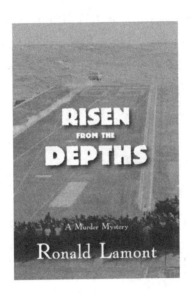

- PROLOGUE -

His eyelids... he can't seem to force them open... like a bad dream where you want to wake up, but you can't.

He tries to speak. A low moan is all that he can muster.

He summons every ounce of strength to open his eyes – to awaken from the nightmare.

A faint glimmer of muted light seeps in. A semblance of reality appears, but the vista is perplexing...

"What's that in front of me? It looks like the end of a road, but there's nothing but boundless sky beyond it? Wait... that's not the sky... that's water... everywhere. Am I at the edge of a washed-out bridge? Am I trapped in the middle of a flood??"

His head suddenly snaps back...

1

A thirty year-old 76-foot fishing trawler bobs and weaves like a prizefighter on the waters of the mid-Pacific ocean.

The boat's winches whine as they struggle to haul in the day's catch.

The net breaks the surface and is lifted high by the winch and crane. The size of the load catches many of the crewmen off-guard... envisioning 'dollar signs' as a result of their biggest catch in weeks.

Observing the hovering load a crewman turns to the Captain and proclaims, "Holy crap Cap, we've hit the Mother Lode!"

The seasoned Captain knows better and chuckles to himself, "Ah, the optimistic naiveté of a rookie."

"Don't count your pay just yet there Duncan," responds the Captain, "for all we know we could be hauling-in a giant squid or some other Denizen of the Deep that's not a part of the menu, payload that broke loose from a cargo ship during a storm, or a big pile of trash from a cruise ship."

A few crewmen guide the load down to the deck.

"Something made a hard landing," replies one of the crewmen.

"I hope we're not looking at the proverbial *'boot hanging from the end of a fishing pole'*," says another in response.

The net falls away and an avalanche of fish spew across the deck, revealing an unexpected captive to the astonished crew... a 1960's era automobile.

The Captain is as surprised as the rest of the crew and mumbles under his breath, "That's neither the lost payload nor pile of trash I had in mind."

A closer look at 'the catch' reveals an unusual paint job - not unlike that of a military fighter jet, right down to a squadron insignia and the lettering *U.S. NAVY.*

Several of the crewmen approach the vehicle in a manner similar to a Sheriff approaching an abandoned car on a remote dirt road... a mixture of curiosity and trepidation.

The Captain approaches the passenger-side windows in an attempt to peer inside for a glimpse of the car's bounty, alas the windows are darkened with sea-growth.

One of the crewmen grabs the driver's-side door handle and tries to open the door - nothing. He takes a deep breath, tightens his grip, and follows with a hard yank.

The car door flings open and the crewman falls to the deck... gallons of fish and water cascading over him.

"Son of a bitch!" yells the crewman.

As the waterfall recedes he notices a body, sprawled half out of the door but held in place by the lap belt. The body is clad in an aviator's flight suit; a pilot helmet askew atop his head.

"What the fuck?" the crewman says as he picks himself up from the deck, flaps his arms and hands to shake off the water, and heads toward the body.

"Somebody's screwin' with us," he yells to the Captain, "there's a freakin' dummy behind the wheel!"

A closer look seems to confirm his suspicion... besides the flight suit the 'dummy' is wearing gloves, *"Surely to cover up mannequin hands,"* the crewman thinks to himself. And the head is conveniently covered by the helmet with its visor down in order to hide his *mannequin eyes.*

"Oh here we go," the crewman says aloud in a confirming manner as he notices the 'pilot' is wearing a mask... a strange, almost human-like Halloween mask.

He raises the helmet's visor to get a closer look. As the visor passes the eyes the cavernous sockets reveal a grisly, semi-fleshy, skull.

The crewman jumps back in surprise and disgust.

"Holy Fuck!" he says as he looks toward the Captain, "We've got a problem."

CPSIA information can be obtained
at www.ICGtesting.com
Printed in the USA
BVHW04s0921031018
529149BV00019B/1194/P